Spellbound

ALSO BY ANNA DALE

Whispering to Witches
Dawn Undercover

Spellbound

Anna Dale

BLOOMSBURY
CHILDREN'S
BOOKS

First published in Great Britain by Bloomsbury Publishing Plc
Published in the United States by Bloomsbury U.S.A. Children's Books
175 Fifth Avenue, New York, New York 10010
Distributed to the trade by Macmillan

Library of Congress Cataloging-in-Publication Data
Dale, Anna.
Spellbound / by Anna Dale. — 1st U.S. ed.
p.   cm.
Summary: A quiet summer vacation in a small country village
turns out to be anything but peaceful for Athene and her younger
brother, Zach, when they find themselves caught up in a skirmish
between two groups of magical, gnome-like creatures.
ISBN-13: 978-1-59990-006-3 • ISBN-10: 1-59990-006-8
[1. Magic—Fiction. 2. Brothers and sisters—Fiction.] I. Title.
PZ7.D15225Sp 2008   [Fic]—dc22   2007052115

First U.S. Edition 2008
Typeset by Dorchester Typesetting Group Ltd
Printed in the U.S.A. by Quebecor World Fairfield
2 4 6 8 10 9 7 5 3 1

All papers used by Bloomsbury U.S.A. are natural, recyclable products
made from wood grown in well-managed forests. The manufacturing processes
conform to the environmental regulations of the country of origin.

To Mole Coleman, Jo Galpin and Kerry Kelsey

Chapter One

West to freshwater

It goes without saying that brothers and sisters often share things with each other, like knock knees, turned-up noses, freckles, the measles, and – if they are kind and generous – toys and bags of sweets; but apart from sharing the same father and mother, Athene and Zachary Enright, aged twelve and six respectively, didn't share anything *at all*.

To start with, they looked as completely unalike as a panda and a porcupine. Athene had a sheet of dark brown hair that she wore tucked neatly behind her ears or braided into the tidiest plait that you have ever seen, whereas her younger brother, Zach, looked as if he had daubed his head with glue and stuck it in a hayrick. Blonder than custard, his hair was always in a state no matter how often his mother tried to tame it with a comb. Athene was tall and thin and Zach was small and stocky. Bookish and something of a know-it-all, Athene excelled at school in almost every subject whilst Zach was inattentive and more of a sporty, adventurous type.

Zach's nature was as sunny as a day in June, which was when he had been delivered into the world. Athene, on the other hand, had been born on a December night, slap-bang in the middle of a howling gale and her stormy moods and strong will reflected it.

No two siblings could have been so dissimilar as Athene and Zach. They were as distinct from each other as chalk is from cheese. Even their names were at opposite ends of the alphabet.

Of course, there are some people who have nothing at all in common and yet can get along extremely well. Regrettably, this was not the case with the two Enright children. Athene detested her brother from the minute she set eyes on him, wrapped in a white blanket, in his crib on the Katherine ward of Watford General Hospital. Baby Zachary George had done nothing in particular to invoke his sister's deep-seated hatred (at the age of three hours old he could barely do anything but blink). It was the very fact of his existence that she found so maddening – and, from that moment, she promised herself that she would behave as unpleasantly towards him as she could.

By the age of twelve, Athene's spiteful treatment of her brother had become second nature to her. If Zach turned on the television, she switched channels immediately; if they played snakes and ladders together she cheated like crazy to make sure that she won; if they both wanted the last chocolate biscuit on the plate she would give him a pinch to make him change his mind.

On the morning of the third of March, which was a Saturday, the Enright family were to be found in the living room of their home in Chorleywood, leafing through a stack of glossy catalogues, discussing where they would like to spend their summer holiday.

'I want to go camping,' said Zach.

'Do you, dear?' said Mrs Enright nervously. She did not like the thought of sleeping outdoors where there were creepy-crawlies and funny smells. She also had an irrational fear of zips.

'I hate camping,' Athene said with a frown.

'What about a boating holiday?' said Mr Enright keenly. 'A week on a canal in Worcestershire sounds nice.'

'Yeah, let's go on a boat!' said Zach. 'A big one with a red sail!' He bounced up and down excitedly on the sofa.

'I hate boats,' said Athene, scowling hard.

Eventually, they settled upon two weeks in a farmhouse in Somerset, which offered Bed and Breakfast. Athene was the one to suggest it. She found a picture of the farmhouse in a catalogue which told her to 'While Away the Summer in the West Country'. Her attention was grabbed by the colour of the farmhouse's front door. She wasn't especially fond of the colour itself but she *was* extremely proud of knowing what it was called.

'It's viridian,' she told everybody smugly. She always took great pleasure in using long, unusual words, never wanting to miss an opportunity to demonstrate how smart she was.

'What a lovely farmhouse – and it's in Somerset!' said Mrs Enright delightedly. She had been on holiday there when she was a girl and had spent many happy hours cycling through its countryside.

'This house has got a croquet lawn and a tennis court!' said Mr Enright who always packed his training shoes when he went away. He liked to keep himself in trim.

'And a pond!' exclaimed Zach.

They were planning to go there in the first two weeks in August, which was, reputedly, the hottest time of the year. With any luck, thought Athene slyly, by the time that we've arrived, the pond will have dried up.

She had no idea as she sat there, gloating because she had succeeded in getting her own way, that this year's summer holiday would turn out to be the most thrilling and, by far, the most dangerous that she had ever had.

On the fourth of August, the Enright family got up bright and early and piled into their car. The journey from Chorleywood to Somerset was long and hot and not without moments of tension. Athene and Zach sat next to each other in the back seat for three-and-a-half torturous hours and when they drove past a sign for the village of Mistlebrook and pulled up in the driveway of Freshwater Farmhouse, Athene felt so relieved that she almost gave a hearty cheer. She had barely waited for the wheels to stop turning before she undid her seatbelt and scrambled eagerly out of the car.

The farmhouse was three times the size of their house back in Chorleywood. It had the lumpy, lopsided look of somewhere very old. Athene was pleased to see that its door was the same shade of bluish-green as it had been in the photograph. As she watched, the door opened and a dog tumbled out of it, followed by a woman who looked nothing like the type of farmer's wife that Athene had read about in books. What was this woman doing in flip-flops, a pair of shorts and a halter-neck top? Where were her galoshes, her apron and her ruddy cheeks? What on earth was she thinking of?

Despite her unauthentic wardrobe, the woman proved to be rather nice. Her name was Mrs Virginia Stirrup.

'But you can call me Ginnie,' she told them.

Ginnie looked over sixty and was slimmer than a reed, yet she hoicked two suitcases out of the boot of the Enrights' car with no trouble at all.

Trying not to trip over her portly black labrador

whose name, rather aptly, was Podge, the Enrights followed Ginnie into the farmhouse. Passing through the living room was like perusing the stalls at a jumble sale. There were pictures, board games and jigsaws, and books in untidy, precarious piles. In the furthest corner of the room was a table with four chairs placed around it which was where the guests were served their home-cooked breakfasts. Beyond the table and chairs was a wide, carpeted staircase which they climbed to get to the guest bedrooms in the west wing.

All hell broke loose when Athene discovered that there were only two of them.

'I'm not sharing a room with Zach,' Athene informed her parents.

Mr and Mrs Enright did their best to persuade their obstinate daughter to change her mind, but they met with stiff resistance.

'I don't mind sleeping in the bathroom,' said Athene. 'It'd be quite cosy, I expect. I could bed down in the bathtub.'

'Don't be ridiculous,' said her dad. 'Why do you have to make such a fuss? Sharing a room with your brother isn't that much of a hardship, surely.'

'I'd rather sleep outside,' said Athene, steely-eyed and determined. 'I'd *rather* sleep on the *moon*.'

In the end, she got what she wanted. It was decided that Zach would move into their parents' room and share with them for the next two weeks. Ginnie lugged a camp bed upstairs, single-handedly, and put it in a corner of their bedroom.

Athene was relieved and delighted to be sleeping in a room on her own. Hers was a large, grand, grown-up sort of bedroom with tapestries, dark furniture and a chandelier.

After the Enrights had unpacked, they went downstairs and sat on one of the big old sofas in the living room. Over a glass of lemonade and a freshly baked macaroon, Ginnie told them all about the history of Freshwater Farmhouse. It was built in the 1500s, but the Stirrups had only lived in it for ninety of the intervening years, starting with Ishmael Stirrup who had bought the house for a meagre sum from a pair of dotty old ladies called Ada and Fredegond Cheese.

'We like to think of them as Gouda and Cheddargond,' said Ginnie, grinning broadly. She pointed to a framed picture of the pair, which was hanging on the wall beneath an oil painting. The sisters were old and jowly and their ample figures were dressed prudishly in black bombazine. Neither sister was smiling. 'People didn't say "cheese" in those days, not even if it was their surname!' said Ginnie with a giggle.

Athene didn't think that there was much to chuckle about when she heard the reason behind the sisters' hasty sale. Apparently the Cheeses had sold up in a hurry after having witnessed something very odd one night, which seemed to have convinced them that the old farm-house was haunted.

'You mean they saw a ghost?' said Athene.

There had been no mention of spectral residents in the holiday catalogue. If Athene had known that Freshwater Farmhouse was haunted she may not have been quite so madly keen to stay in it.

'Don't worry, sweetie,' Ginnie said, idly stroking a tabby cat that had jumped on to her lap. 'There's nothing to be scared of. There are no ghosts here. Never heard so much as a groan or a rattling chain. Those Cheese sisters were seeing things, if you ask me. A right doolally pair they were, by all accounts.'

Athene took a sneaky sideways glance at her brother to see if he had been frightened by Ginnie's talk of ghosts. Perhaps, when night-time came, she could wrap a bed sheet around herself and pretend she was a spook to give him a scare.

Disappointingly, Zach did not appear to have been listening to anything that had been said. He had brought his coloured pens and drawing pad downstairs and was scribbling away to his heart's content. She watched as he drew a stick figure with mad, spidery hands and a very long dress, and then another and then another until he had filled a whole page. Athene smirked. Zach was not much good at art. Very tall ladies were all that he could draw. He never drew *anything* else.

The plate of macaroons had been emptied by the time that Ginnie had finished telling them about all the Stirrups who had lived at the farm. Ginnie's husband Jonathan (known as Jonnie) was the great-grandson of Ishmael. Jonnie had inherited the house a quarter of a century ago and he and Ginnie had brought up a son and two daughters, all of whom had flown the nest. Jonnie had been an architect but nowadays he kept himself occupied by dabbling in farming. It had been Ginnie's idea to start up the Bed and Breakfast business because, in her opinion, the farmhouse was far too big for two and, with her children gone, there was nobody left to make a fuss of.

'Apart from your cat,' Athene pointed out.

'Yes, she's a dear,' said Ginnie, smiling fondly at the tabby who was curled up on her knees. 'Her name is Crumbs. We got her from a neighbour who brought her round in a biscuit tin. An empty one, I hasten to add. That's why we called her Crumbs, you see.'

Aside from Crumbs and their labrador, Podge, the Stirrups owned a cow, three pigs, two goats, and several hens and ducks.

'All of whom need feeding,' Ginnie told her guests with a sigh. She lifted the sleepy cat from her lap and got to her feet. 'You'll excuse me, won't you, while I see to my menagerie?'

The Enrights had their evening meal in The Stag and Pheasant, a pub which was a ten-minute car-ride from the farm, in a village called Owlet Corner. Athene ordered toad-in-the-hole to be followed by apricot pie. The gravy was too thick and the piecrust burnt but she ate her dinner quietly, without a fuss. After she had won the fight to have a bedroom of her own, she had been warned not to step out of line for the rest of the day. If she did not behave well enough from now until bedtime, it was highly likely that she would receive a punishment. There had been talk of a bicycle ride the next morning and she did not want to risk missing out on such a lovely treat.

When they returned to Freshwater Farm, they were all worn out after their eventful day and, sticking to her plan to be good, Athene made no objection when she was advised to go to bed at half past eight.

'Goodnight, Eeny,' said Zach. Her brother had always called her 'Eeny'. He hadn't been able to get his tongue around 'Athene' as a toddler. Eeny had been the best that he could manage and now that he was six and quite capable of saying her name properly, he stuck steadfastly to its shortened form. Athene reckoned that he only did it to get on her nerves. Just lately, her father had taken to calling her by this name as well or, worse, Eeny Meeny Miny Mo, which was ten times more humiliating.

'Night, dung breath,' Athene said, in a voice that was far too hushed for her parents to overhear.

Zach giggled. He did not seem to mind when she called him by a nasty name. Any normal brother would cry or stick his tongue out or say something horrible in return – but not Zachary Enright. His happy-go-lucky attitude was a constant source of irritation to Athene. It took quite an effort to think of hurtful things to call him – and sometimes she thought that it wasn't worth the bother.

Alone in her bedroom, Athene put on her nightdress and switched on her bedside lamp. She sat cross-legged on her bed and wrote down the day's events in her diary, which she did, habitually, every night. Her diary entry completed, she crossed the floor to close the curtains. They were made from a heavy material and she found it a struggle to drag the curtain rings along the poles. The room had three enormous windows and Athene abandoned her task in the end. There was no need to draw them completely in any case. The farmhouse was several miles from the nearest village of Mistlebrook and all that the windows looked out upon were lawns and fields at the front of the house and a walled garden at the rear. Athene watched from a window, confident that no human eye could see her standing there. The driveway stretched eel-like towards the nearest road.

Athene climbed back into bed and put out the light.

There is something very unnerving about being alone in a strange room in the dark and although the sun had not quite set, and in spite of the fact that Athene wasn't easily scared, she felt the need to pull the bedclothes right up to her chin. She lay underneath them very stiffly for the next five minutes. It was far too quiet. There were no noises coming from her parents' room or from the fields and gardens outside. The only sound that she could hear was the thump-thump-thump of her heart.

Athene wasn't sure if she believed in ghosts or not. It depended at what hour of the day she was asked for her opinion. At half past four in the afternoon, in a room full of people, as she was preparing to help herself to her third macaroon, she might say that they probably didn't exist but if she was asked at a quarter to nine in the evening, just before nightfall, it was quite likely that she would have changed her mind.

The Cheese sisters had been sufficiently spooked to sell their house for next to nothing and move out of Somerset altogether, whereas Ginnie and Jonnie had lived in the farmhouse for twenty-five years and had not seen a ghost in all that time. Who was Athene to believe?

She felt chilled suddenly. Was there a draught? Had

she left a window open? Did a curtain billow just then? Her heart thumped very fast. She'd never get to sleep at this rate. What on earth was she to do?

There was no little brother to call out to. She had taken great pains to ensure that she had this bedroom all to herself – and there wasn't a favourite teddy bear or doll to hug in her arms. Now that she had started secondary school, Athene had told herself that she was far too old for such childish things.

If she knocked on the door of her parents' room and told them that she didn't like being on her own she would probably be torn limb from limb and the cycle ride tomorrow would most certainly be off. Perhaps she could find a soft toy of some sort downstairs. There had been board games and jigsaws in the living room so perhaps there were a few soft toys too. Or – even better than a toy – she could track down a live animal. Podge was too excitable and he'd probably take up half the bed – but Crumbs the cat was small and furry and likely to be as warm as toast. Pigs and goats were not even worth considering. Athene's mind was made up. Crumbs would be just perfect. With a comforting presence like Crumbs curled up next to her, a good night's sleep would be guaranteed. Without further ado, she threw back her bedclothes, put on her slippers and went off in search of the Stirrups' cat.

There were rooms in the house where guests were

allowed to roam and other rooms that were not to be strayed into unless you were a Stirrup. Athene looked in them all. She even dared to peek into the kitchen where Ginnie and Jonnie were drinking tea and listening to a concert on the radio. It was Athene's first glimpse of Jonnie Stirrup. She noted that he had hay stalks in his hair and was wearing an old holey jumper. Podge was in the kitchen too. He was the only one to see Athene peeping through a crack in the door. Luckily for her, Podge was half asleep and could not rouse his bones to get out of his basket and greet her. A cocked ear and a couple of whirls of his tail was all that he could muster.

'Drat!' said Athene quietly. The kitchen had been her last hope. Well, perhaps, there was *one* more place she hadn't looked . . .

Once she had unbolted the back door of the farm-house, she stepped out into the garden. Through her slippers she felt every lump in the ground as she ventured over the grass. It was a pleasant summer's evening: warm and still, and she soon found that she wasn't the only one to be out and about in it. She encountered moths and a hedgehog, snails and two rabbits, nibbling at Mr Stirrup's lettuces; and finally she came across the most amazing creature of all.

Chapter Two

An Invitation to Breakfast

'Crumbs?' said Athene. 'Crumbs, is that you?'

The sun had already dropped out of sight like a penny in a slot and the coppery gleam it had left behind in the clouds was nearly gone. Dusk was threatening to fall and Athene was finding it harder to see. She moved closer to the fence that marked the boundary between the Stirrups' well-kept lawn and the tall, tousled grasses which grew unchecked in the meadow beyond.

Something was moving slowly across a corner of the field.

Athene stared harder and called Crumbs' name again but the creature did not respond or change its course. The light was too poor and the distance too far to be sure that the shadowy shape was Crumbs the cat. Athene hitched up her nightdress, flung her leg over the fence and jumped down into the field. There was nothing else for it. She'd have to get a closer look.

As she ran towards it, the creature seemed to quicken its pace but its speed was feeble compared with Athene's. After she had run a hundred paces or so, Athene realised that the animal was far too big to be a cat. This was a blow but, by now, she was too curious to contemplate giving up the chase. When she had covered another fifty metres of the field, she was able to see that the creature had two legs. It was a person! – and a very short one at that. *Probably a child*, thought Athene, squinting in the gloom. But what a small child was doing all alone in a field in the dark, she could not even begin to guess. And where had he come from? The nearest village was several miles away.

It must be a stupid child, she said to herself. *A stupid little numbskull who's gone and got himself lost.*

Athene rolled her eyes. Why hadn't she thought of him before?

'Zach!' she shouted. 'Zach, you idiot! Wait!'

She drew close enough to see that he was limping. Given that he'd injured his leg, it was hardly surprising that she'd caught him up so easily. What on earth could her brother be doing out here? It was a strange time of day to go exploring.

Athene had no idea how Zach had sneaked out of her parents' room or quite how he had managed to get outside (the bolts on the back door had been drawn across), but she did know that he was about to get in a whole heap of trouble for it.

Athene planned it out in her head. When she had caught hold of Zach, she would march him back to the farmhouse and wake her parents up. She would tell them how she had happened to glance out of her bedroom window and seen Zach haring off on one of his rambles. Worried about his welfare, she had rushed outside after him and brought him safely back. She would be praised and Zach would get a ticking off. How could a day end more perfectly than that?

The shoulder that she grabbed was clad in thick, lumpy wool and not the cotton fabric of a pyjama top. This should have been enough to warn Athene that she was in for a very big shock.

'What *are* you?' she said, when she had finished screaming.

The little man in front of her uncovered his ears. He did not look at all pleased.

'What am I?' he said. 'I'll tell you what I am, my dear. I'm lucky not to have been deafened by your screeching. Wherever did you learn to make a noise like that?'

'Sorry,' said Athene. 'You startled me.'

The man, who was at least a head shorter than Athene, gave a brief, incredulous snort. 'If anyone's been doing any startling – it's you. Chasing after me, calling me names and pulling me about . . . No manners, that's your trouble, my dear.'

'I thought you were my brother,' she said.

'Do I look like him?' said the man. 'Well, do I?'

'No,' Athene said. 'Not at all.' In fact, the man did not resemble anyone she knew. He was the oddest person that she had ever come across. His skin was striped and speckled, his eyes shone like pearl buttons and his broad, bat-like ears were inclined to flap and twitch. 'I couldn't see you properly until I got up close. It's too dark,' she explained.

'Yes, for your kind it is,' said the man with a grin, 'but not for mine.'

'What is your kind, exactly?' asked Athene.

'I'm human, same as you. Only I'm a Gloam and you're a Glare.'

'I beg your pardon?' said Athene.

'Slow on the uptake are you?' he said.

Athene glowered at him. 'I'm very quick at catching on if people bother to explain things properly,' she told him.

'No need to take that tone,' said the man. 'Very well, I'll do my best to put it as plainly as I can. There are two types of human being, not one as you might have been led to believe. The Gloam are nocturnal. That means . . .'

'I know what it means,' interrupted Athene. 'You're awake at night whereas the other kind – my kind – are active during the day. I get it.'

'May I continue?' asked the man in a haughty voice.

'Yes,' Athene said. 'Please do.'

'Although we are the same species, there are many differences between the Gloam and the Glare,' said the man. 'We Gloam can see superbly well in the dark, our hearing is exceptional, and we choose to live peaceably in secluded groups in the countryside. You Glare, on the other hand, can only see with the aid of bright light, your hearing is poor, you are big and fat, loud and incredibly nosy.'

'And you're very rude,' said Athene, amazed at the man's impertinence. 'You've got no right to say those things. Just like you've no right to be in this field. What are you doing here anyway? This land belongs to the Stirrups. You're trespassing, you know!'

'I was merely collecting some dandelions, heartsease and ox-eye daisies,' said the man, patting a bag which rested against his hip. 'I believe you Glare refer to them as weeds. Now, if you don't mind I mustn't loiter for a moment more. Breakfast is always served a half-hour after sundown and it's almost that time now. Well, so long!' he said cheerfully, turning to go. 'I can't say it's been a pleasure to meet you, but it's certainly not been a bore.'

'You can't leave!' Athene told him. 'I want to know more about you. You've hardly told me anything!' She was extremely annoyed that the man intended to disappear before he had shared every single grain of his knowledge. She hated people knowing more than she did.

'I simply must be off,' said the man and he started to limp away from her. 'Go home to bed, my dear, where you belong.'

'Wait!' Athene pleaded, trailing after him. 'Couldn't I come with you? If you were any sort of gentleman, you'd invite me to share a bite of your breakfast.' To her surprise, she felt her stomach clench. Walking in the fresh air had given her an appetite. The toad-in-the-hole and apricot pie that she had enjoyed in the pub seemed an awfully long time ago.

'Please!' she said imploringly. 'I've never met a Gloam before and I think . . . I think you're rather wonderful.'

Athene heard the man sigh. He turned his shining eyes in her direction and she felt them studying her with renewed interest.

'We're not supposed to hobnob with the Glare,' said the man. 'I've got nothing against you personally: you're quite annoying, but not unbearably so. It's the others, you see . . . they're not used to visitors. If I turned up to breakfast with a Glare as my guest, it would cause a sensation.' He smiled briefly and the eagerness in his voice betrayed a change of heart. 'You and I would be the talk of the tribe and your arrival would impress my little friend, Huffkin, no end. She's very curious about the Glare. She's particularly taken with those sculptures of yours.'

Athene sensed that the man's resolve was weakening. 'What sculptures?' she asked.

The man pointed to a great tower of metal which was silhouetted against the evening sky.

'They're not sculptures,' said Athene. 'They're called pylons. They hold up electric cables. You know what electricity is, don't you?'

'Naturally,' said the man, but Athene was unconvinced that he was telling the truth.

'OK, here's the deal,' she said boldly. 'I'll tell you about electricity if you invite me to breakfast.'

'Agreed,' said the man after a lengthy pause. 'It's simple fare, but you're welcome to a frog and dandelion sandwich and a cup of brew.' He offered her his arm.

Athene hesitated. She had badgered the man until he had relented, but now that he had asked her to breakfast she found that she was a little nervous about going with him. He was a total stranger and he had also asked her to share a meal that sounded extremely unappetising. However, he seemed like a decent enough fellow and she was desperate to meet some more of the mysterious Gloam.

She took his arm and smiled at him. 'My name is Athene,' she said.

'And I'm Humdudgeon,' responded the man. 'It's not

too far, Athene. Just a few fields away. I do hope the others will welcome you. We've never entertained a Glare before.'

'Ooh!' said Athene. Her skin prickled uncomfortably. Unable to see where she was going, she had staggered into some nettles. 'Where on earth are you taking me, Humdudgeon?' she grumbled. 'Those blasted nettles have stung me. Ouch, it hurts like anything.'

'So sorry,' said Humdudgeon, guiding her away from the beds of stinging nettles. 'I forgot to warn you. We Gloam can pass through the nettles unscathed, but you Glare seem to break out in painful bumps whenever you touch the hairs on the leaves. That's why we picked this spot to set up camp. We sleep in the nettles by day and no one ever bothers us. When night falls we creep out and gather in the clearing which is up ahead. You'll be meeting my tribe in a minute or two. Ah, we've been spotted. Here's the friend I was telling you about . . .'

Two pinpricks of light glided towards them accompanied by the patter of feet.

'She looks thrilled to her toes to see you,' said Humdudgeon. He grasped Athene by the elbow and steered her past a shadowy shape which Athene guessed was another nettle bed.

'Hello!' said a breathless voice.

'Oh, hi there,' said Athene, sucking the little raised spots on her hands. 'I don't suppose you've got such a thing as a first-aid kit?'

No sooner had she spoken than a hand about the same size as a child's pressed a cool, moist leaf to the sore places on Athene's skin. It had a wonderfully soothing effect.

'Dock leaves have healing powers,' said Humdudgeon's friend.

'Thanks. It feels much better. I'm Athene. What's your name?' Athene asked.

'I'm Huffkin,' replied the Gloam in an awestruck voice. Athene squinted in the darkness and managed to make out a heart-shaped face and a crown of bushy hair. Before she and Huffkin could say another word to each other, Athene heard shrill exclamations in the distance and saw dozens of shining dots moving this way and that. A thunderous drumming sound reached her ears as the whole of Humdudgeon's tribe approached to meet their new visitor. They halted in a semicircle in front of her. The Gloam's eyes seemed to flash at intervals, vanishing for a fraction of a second before reappearing again. It seemed as if they were signalling to each other, but after a few moments, Athene realised that they were merely blinking.

The Gloam's raucous chattering quietened to a dull murmur and somebody stepped forward. Athene heard their heavy tread and saw their eyes floating in the air to her right, just in front of where Humdudgeon was standing. In the darkness she could just glimpse a beefy figure with broad shoulders and a jutting chin.

'What is the meaning of this?' demanded the person angrily.

'Don't upset yourself, Chief. She's a friend,' Humdudgeon said calmly. 'Her name is Athene. We met tonight in the meadow where the salad flowers grow. She wanted to meet us all, so I asked her to join us for breakfast.'

There were gasps of amazement and yells of consternation. There was also a lot of nervous tittering and, cutting through all this noise, an elderly female voice demanded none too politely to know what was going on.

'Gloam do not befriend Glare!' said the Chief. 'You know as well as I do what the Glare are like. They are far too meddlesome. Our ancestors decided centuries ago that we shouldn't have anything to do with them and that's the way it's going to stay. You think you know better than our ancestors, do you? If the Glare found out that we existed they wouldn't leave us alone. They'd hunt us down and put us in cages and charge a fortune for the privilege of taking a peek at us. No, no. The

Gloam and Glare are too different. We can never be friends.'

Although Athene did not say as much, she thought that the Chief was probably right. She wasn't sure if the Glare would be allowed to imprison the Gloam. In this day and age, there was bound to be some law against that sort of thing, but the Gloam would undoubtedly be hounded by the press and pestered by documentary film makers and they'd almost certainly be forced by the government to go to school and get real jobs and pay taxes and other mundane things. In short: their lives would be ruined.

'She's only a youngster,' Humdudgeon protested. 'She doesn't mean us any harm. Huffkin and I will take charge of her. She won't be any bother at all.'

Athene smiled winsomely at the sea of pearly eyes.

'Let her stay for a while!' someone shouted. 'We've never seen a Glare up close!'

Athene's smile grew wider. She heard the Chief grunt and saw him shake his head dejectedly.

'Oh, very well,' he conceded with reluctance. He stuck out his hand and gripped Athene's palm. 'The name's Pucklepod. Welcome to the Humble tribe.'

'Thank you,' said Athene.

There were groans and mumblings, but also a few wolf whistles and cheers from the crowd. Athene felt her chest swelling with pride. Then the Chief leaned closer so that she felt his bristly beard rub against her cheek.

'Make sure you behave yourself,' he muttered, 'or your visit will be a very short one.'

Chapter Three

Goggle Drops

Under a gibbous moon, which glowed like a white pebble, and stars that were scattered in the sky like grains of sand, Athene sat at the edge of the clearing between the dim forms of Huffkin and Humdudgeon. She held a wooden goblet in her hands.

It was now so dark that Athene's eyes were almost useless. She could see blocks of shadow and the outlines of people and, of course, the shining specks that were the Gloam's eyes. It did not matter so much that she could not see very well; thanks to her other senses she was still able to comprehend what was happening around her.

Over the past half-hour or so, her hands had been shaken umpteen times and the same smooth, cold fingers which had grasped her palms, had touched her hair and brushed her skin. She had been fussed over and marvelled at and asked a whole host of questions. Her inquisitors had ranged from the very young to the exceptionally old ('I'm eighty-three,' a lady called Dottle had told her on no less than seven occasions). The whole experience had given Athene an inkling of what it must be like to be a creature in a zoo or an actress at a film premiere. When all the poking and prodding and questioning had got too much, Humdudgeon and Huffkin had shooed all the Gloam away.

True to his word, Humdudgeon had taken good care of Athene, and Huffkin, his friend, had been equally as kind. The two Gloam had sat her down on one of their chairs, which felt distinctly like a tree stump, and given her a drink of 'brew', which tasted like cold tea.

Athene raised the goblet to her lips and sipped the drink dreamily.

'Would you care for a moth wing crisp?' said Huffkin in her light, high voice. She seemed most determined to persuade Athene to eat something.

'No, thanks,' Athene said, which had been her answer earlier when offered newt soup, a frog sandwich and a snail kebab. 'Have you ever tried Glare food?' Athene asked. 'Chocolate is the best. It tastes really sweet and it melts into a sort of gloop on your tongue. Our crisps are delicious too. We have hundreds of different flavours. Then there's exotic fruit. My favourite is the kumquat. Well, I've never actually tasted it, but it's got an awesome name. Oh! We're taking a picnic lunch to the beach tomorrow. I don't suppose your chief would let you come along? I'm sure my mum and dad wouldn't mind . . .'

'We'd be a little too conspicuous,' Humdudgeon reminded her. 'Not to mention the fact that the sunlight would blister our skin and probably blind us as well.'

'Oh, yes. Of course . . . I'm sorry,' Athene mumbled. She told them that she was tired and therefore her brain was working sluggishly, but the truth was that, in the darkness, she had forgotten how very different the Gloam were from the Glare.

'It was a nice thought,' said Huffkin, patting Athene's arm. 'Now, if you're sure you've had enough to eat and drink, we'd better get you home.'

Huffkin and Humdudgeon escorted her across the fields to make sure that she got back to the farmhouse without losing her way. Before they parted company, they all agreed to meet up the following evening under the tallest tree at the north end of the Stirrups' front garden. To Athene's delight, the two Gloam promised to bring her a 'surprise'.

Athene continued to gaze out of her bedroom window long after her new friends had scooted across the front lawn and disappeared into the darkness. It had been such a thrilling evening and she could not wait to see them again. The next twenty hours were bound to crawl by which, in her experience, was what tended to happen when you were particularly looking forward to something.

Before going to sleep, she tried to add a bit about the Gloam to her diary entry for the fourth of August but her pens kept running out of ink. The next day she was frustrated again, when, after breakfast, she cornered Ginnie by the kitchen door and tried to ask her if she knew about the Gloam. Every time that she opened her mouth the words would not come out.

'Are you feeling quite all right, Athene?' Ginnie said. 'Perhaps you should sit down for a minute. I'll bring you a glass of water.'

Athene was baffled by these two peculiar incidents. She puzzled over them for almost the entire day: on their six-mile cycle ride, in the car on the way to Brean Sands, during her swim, as she walked along the beach to fetch ice creams, while she was sitting watching Zach build a sandcastle (which she 'accidentally' kicked over shortly afterwards). By teatime, Athene thought that she might have finally figured it out.

That evening, her parents seemed to stay up for ages, playing a game called backgammon in the living room. At last, they went to bed and no sooner had they shut their bedroom door and turned out their light, than Athene bolted downstairs, fully dressed, and hastened to where she had arranged to meet her two Gloam friends. Humdudgeon and Huffkin were waiting under the tree. They began to tell her something in excited voices but

Athene interrupted them.

'Why didn't you think to mention that you could do magic?' she said.

Huffkin and Humdudgeon exchanged guilty glances.

'It's not as if it's anything special,' Humdudgeon said airily. 'After all, the Glare can do it, too. Look at your horseless carriages and flying machines and funny little boxes with pictures inside . . .'

'That's not magic,' Athene snapped. 'It's science. Remember what I told you about electricity? The only Glare magicians are people in white gloves who pull rabbits out of hats and stupid things like that. They do tricks – not magic. Not *real* magic like *you*.' Athene gave the two Gloam a very stern look. 'What was that spell you put on me? You could have asked first. It's not very nice being magicked, you know.'

'It was Pucklepod! He made us do it!' said Huffkin.

'We had no choice,' Humdudgeon said. 'If any of us meet a Glare we have to make sure that they won't breathe a word to another soul. How do you think we've survived in secret all these years?'

'You should have got me to promise,' said Athene sulkily.

'Too risky, my dear,' Humdudgeon said. 'The spell takes care of everything. It stops you from talking about us . . .'

'And writing,' Athene said. 'My pens ran out of ink!'

'Please don't be cross with us,' Huffkin said beseech-ingly. She slipped her little hand in the crook of Athene's arm.

Athene softened. She could see that the two Gloam had acted for the good of their kind. Even if she'd promised to keep quiet about them she mightn't have been able to keep her word. 'I suppose I forgive you,' she said.

Just then, a light came on in one of the upstairs rooms of the farmhouse. The two Gloam ducked behind the tree and Athene copied them. Then all three ran towards the fence and wriggled through it. They walked across the field as nightfall descended. Athene was still fascinat-ed by the Gloam's ability to do magic.

'Now,' she said, 'suppose you tell me what other spells you know?'

'The Humble Gloam don't know much magic at all, really,' Humdudgeon said as he limped along at her side. 'Not like the Low Gloam. Their magic is powerfully strong. You don't want to mess with them.'

'Humdudgeon did,' piped up Huffkin, 'and just look what happened to him!'

'What?' asked Athene. She gave Humdudgeon a nudge.

'I got roughed up a bit,' he said.

'He was knocked about so badly that he could barely walk!' said Huffkin, outraged on her friend's behalf. 'He tried to help a Gloam girl who was being chased by three Low Gloam thugs. To give her a chance to get away, he took on all three of the rascals and got an awful beating. His leg still hasn't healed properly!'

Athene was impressed. 'That took real guts, Humdudgeon.'

'He's a hero!' Huffkin said with more than a hint of pride in her voice. 'The most courageous Gloam this side of Shepton!'

'Come, now,' Humdudgeon muttered. 'I wasn't as brave as all that.'

As the darkness deepened, Athene tripped and stumbled, unable to see where she was placing her feet. She found it hard to keep her balance on the hummocky ground.

'Ow!' she cried as she wrenched her ankle painfully.

'Gosh, I'd quite forgotten,' said Huffkin, patting her pocket. She brought out a pouch made from evergreen leaves. 'Stop a moment, Athene. I've got something here that will make things a whole lot easier for you.'

Humdudgeon rubbed his hands and gave a broad smile. Athene could see the moonlight glinting on his teeth.

'What's that thing?' asked Athene as Huffkin opened the pouch and slid out an object that looked like a small, oval stone. The Gloam woman placed it in Athene's hands.

'It's a shell!' Athene said, feeling the object with her fingers. 'One of those pretty, twirly ones – and there's a piece of cork stuck into it!'

'It's a bottle, actually,' Humdudgeon said, 'and it's got something special inside.'

He took the little shell bottle from her and unplugged it.

'We pinched this,' Humdudgeon said.

'Borrowed it,' said Huffkin. 'Well, old Dottle won't miss a drop or two . . .'

'Do you think you could kneel down?' Humdudgeon asked Athene, 'and put your head right back, my dear, and open your eyes as wide as you can.'

Athene did as she was told. She wasn't at all sure what the Gloam had in store for her, but nevertheless she had no qualms about trusting them.

She gasped as two ice-cold droplets fell into her eyes.

It was an instinctive reaction to blink and, as Athene did, the cool liquid spread to coat the surface of each eye. The feeling was a pleasant one and, what is more, it had the most remarkable effect on her sight. Instead of peering in the dark, and barely managing to recognise a thing, Athene discovered that she could now see as clearly as she could in the daytime; the only difference being that it was all in black and white, just like a piece of film footage from the olden days.

'Wow!' said Athene, getting to her feet. 'That stuff

you just put in my eyes is amazing!' She smiled at the two Gloam and, for the first time, she saw their faces properly. Humdudgeon's was narrow with a long chin and nose, beetling brows and a kindly grin. Huffkin's face was fairer and more delicate; her eyes were merry, her nose pert and her hair was as fluffy as thistledown. Neither Gloam looked over the age of thirty.

'There you are, you see,' Humdudgeon said. 'Being magicked isn't so bad!'

'I suppose not!' said Athene and she laughed. She stared around her at the field of wild grasses, the trees, the hedgerows, and the farmhouse in the distance, all of which she could see perfectly.

'We thought you'd be pleased,' said Huffkin. 'Goggle Drops are wonderful. Our old folk would be lost without them.'

'Why would they be lost?' asked Athene. 'I thought that all Gloam could see in the dark.'

'We're born with good night vision,' explained Huffkin, 'but it tends to fail by the time we've reached old age. A Goggle Drop or two every few hours is all that's needed to keep our sight sharp.'

'Let's explore!' said Athene, linking arms with the two Gloam. It was such an exciting thing to be able to see in the dark and she was eager to take in as much of the night-time landscape as she could. 'Where shall we go?'

'There's a badgers' sett in Moggy Wood,' said

Huffkin. 'There are seven cubs. Badger cubs are fun to watch.'

'Yes! Let's do that!' Athene said. She had seen nature programmes about badgers on TV but she'd never glimpsed a real live badger in the wild. She would have been tempted to break into a run if it hadn't been for Humdudgeon. His lame leg meant that he could only walk at a leisurely pace and, to be polite, she would have to do so too.

On the way to Moggy Wood, they had to cross a country lane. The two Gloam heard the sound of a car long before its headlights appeared over the brow of a hill. By that time, the three friends had hidden their eyes and crouched behind a thick hedge by the roadside. They stayed there until the car and its brash, blinding headlights had streamed safely past.

Athene was the first to squeeze through the hedge and jump out on to the road. Rather than hurry over to the other side, she stood and gazed up and down the narrow lane. It seemed familiar to her.

'I cycled along this road today!' she said to the others as they pushed their way through the thorny hedge. 'I saw a hare in that field over there and just a little further up there's an old tree with a great big hollow trunk. It's half dead, I think, and its branches are all gnarled and twisted. You should see it! Let's nip round the bend and have a look . . .'

'No!' said the two Gloam in unison. They grabbed hold of Athene's arms and stopped her from striding away.

'Why can't we?' Athene asked, struggling to shake them off. (For two slight, diminutive people, their grip was surprisingly strong.) 'It wouldn't take a moment. Ow! Let go!' she said. 'You're pinching me.'

'It's far too risky,' Huffkin said.

''Course it's not!' Athene scoffed. 'There aren't any cars coming.'

'Never mind the traffic,' said Humdudgeon. 'It's the *tree* that's dangerous.'

'Why? What do you mean?' Athene was bewildered. 'How can a *tree* be *dangerous*?' she said.

Chapter four

Roasted and Soaked

'It's not the tree's *fault*,' said Huffkin, still clinging like a clothes peg to Athene's arm. 'Trees are good. At least, I've never met a bad one. It's the fault of the Gloam who have magicked it. *They* have caused the poor tree to be evil.'

'The Low Gloam have made their home in it,' Humdudgeon explained.

'The Low Gloam?' said Athene. 'Oh, aren't they the ones who beat you up?'

'Yes,' said Humdudgeon. He seemed to wince at the memory of it.

'You must have got it wrong,' said Athene lightly. 'You must mean some other tree. The Low Gloam can't be living in *my* tree. It doesn't have any leaves, for a start. They'd be spotted in two seconds if they lounged around in *its* dead branches.'

'They don't live *up* the tree,' Humdudgeon said pointedly. 'Why do you suppose they're called the *Low* Gloam?'

'They live *under* it,' said Huffkin, 'and if you so much as poke your nose inside its trunk, a spell will pull you underground and keep you imprisoned there. It's the strongest sort of spell that can be cast. There's precious little chance of breaking it.'

Athene shivered. 'That can't be true,' she whispered.

Humdudgeon gave a wry smile. 'It's said that the Low Gloam keep you as their servant and work you to the bone until you drop dead. Still want to go and take a look at that tree?' he said, releasing his grip on Athene's arm.

'Er, no . . . perhaps, I don't,' she said, walking the short distance across the lane. She halted by an iron gate and looked ahead to a wooded copse. 'Can we see the badgers, now?' she said.

The next day dawned bright and sunny, but it was also unbearably hot. It was the sweltering kind of heat that makes you feel sticky and uncomfortable and disinclined to move very far. Athene and her mum and dad spent most of it lying in the Stirrups' shady walled garden, sipping cool drinks through a straw and brushing off bugs, which kept alighting on their skin like minute grains of black rice. Zach, who seemed untroubled by the sultry weather, amused himself by running off and then reappearing with a range of different playthings: a croquet mallet, a fishing net, a tennis ball and a handful of felt-tip pens.

At half past four he vanished again only to turn up a few minutes later with Ginnie and a tray in tow. While she held the tray steady, he handed out dishes of vanilla ice cream.

'Thunderbugs,' said Ginnie, when Athene asked her if she knew the name of the pesky insects that had bothered them all day. 'They bring inclement weather. There'll be a thunderstorm before too long, you mark my words.'

The heat and the bugs and the forecast of a downpour put Athene in a really bad mood and when she went into her room to fetch a book and found one of Zach's felt tips lying on her bed, she flew into an almighty rage.

'Zach's been in my room!' she snarled, presenting her parents with the green felt-tip pen. 'He's been snooping about in my things! Tell him that he's not allowed!'

'Zach, old chap,' said Mr Enright to his sheepish-looking son who was skulking behind a deckchair, 'it's not sensible to upset your sister. Better stay out of her room in future, eh?'

'Yes, Dad,' said Zach. 'Sorry.'

'There's a good lad. There's no harm done.'

'Is that *it*?' said Athene, shaking with fury. 'Aren't you going to tell him off *properly*?'

'Did he break anything?' asked Mrs Enright, sitting up on her sun lounger. 'Did he cause any damage to your things?'

'No,' said Athene sulkily.

'Well, then,' said her parents in a way that told her that the matter was closed.

With a livid scowl and with very bad grace, Athene stomped back inside the house.

The evening dragged by just as slowly as the day had done. Athene was desperate for the sun to set because she was meeting the Gloam again. The previous night had been pleasurably spent watching a troupe of badger cubs playing rough and tumble, and tonight, Huffkin and Humdudgeon had promised to take Athene on a moonlit fishing trip.

By nine o'clock, she had changed into her jeans and T-shirt with her swimming costume underneath. She was ready to set off but, worryingly, there were still some bumps and murmurs coming from her parents' room. Athene forced herself to wait. Too het up to write her diary, she paced around the room. Then, when all seemed peaceful next door, she put on her trainers and made her move.

After such a tiresome, frustrating day, Athene was impatient to see the Gloam. She rushed headlong through the house and out into the garden.

'Humdudgeon? Huffkin, are you there?' she called,

having followed the grassy path which led to the front lawn. She drew closer to the sycamore tree, under which they had said they would wait. The ground beneath the tree was shrouded in darkness.

'Hello, Athene,' said Huffkin, emerging from the shadows. She was carrying a sackcloth bag. 'Provisions,' she said, patting its contents, 'and some Goggle Drops for you.'

'Ready for a spot of fishing?' said Humdudgeon cheerfully, stepping into a patch of moonlight. Athene saw that he had three fishing rods strapped to his back and a jar full of worms in his hand. 'Would you mind carrying the bait?' he said.

'Not at all,' said Athene, taking the jar from him. She was relieved to hear that the worms were to be used as bait and weren't Humdudgeon's idea of a tasty midnight snack. She had already learned that the Gloam liked to eat small amphibians and moths and she wouldn't have been surprised to discover that they were partial to worms as well.

'Our canoe is down by the river,' said Huffkin. 'We keep it hidden in a blackberry bush.'

'Great!' Athene said. 'Let's go!'

Hampered by the fishing rods, Humdudgeon was the last of the party to clamber through the fence. Just as he was about to step down into the field, he let out a startled gasp.

'Well, hello,' he said. 'Who's this?'

Athene's vision was misty from the Goggle Drops that Huffkin had tipped into her eyes. Once she had stopped blinking, Athene followed the gaze of her two Gloam friends. She found herself staring at an area of lawn a little to the left of the sycamore tree.

Standing there, in his pyjamas, was a small boy.

'I'm Zach,' he said.

'He's my brother,' Athene growled. She had never in her life been so dismayed to see him. She cursed herself for being so careless. Zach must have heard her on the stairs and got out of bed to see what she was up to. Athene felt almost sick with rage. If the fence had not been between them, she might have grabbed his shoulders and given him a shake.

'Zach, go back to bed!' she told him.

'Must I, Eeny?' he replied. 'Won't you tell me who your friends are first?'

Athene wouldn't, but Humdudgeon and Huffkin were only too willing to introduce themselves.

'What funny names,' said Zach, peering at the Gloam in the darkness. 'Did you say that you were going fishing in a boat? Would there be room for me, do you think?'

'Absolutely not,' Athene said firmly. 'It's a canoe. It wouldn't seat four.'

'I'm sure we could squeeze him in,' said Huffkin. 'He's only a littl'un, after all.'

'Happy to have you along,' Humdudgeon enthused, clapping Zach on the shoulder and helping him over the fence.

'But he's a bit young to be roaming about at night,' said Athene, 'and he can't swim very well . . . and,' she added desperately, 'he's scared of things with scales.' This last statement was a lie.

'Don't worry, Athene,' said Huffkin gently, mistaking Athene's anxiety for genuine concern. 'Your little brother will be safe with us.'

Athene's longest sulking episode had lasted for an hour-and-a-half, but on the night of the fishing expedition she smashed her record to smithereens. She hardly uttered a word when they traipsed together over the fields; she didn't lift a finger to help them drag the canoe from the blackberry bush and launch it in the water; she held on to her fishing rod loosely, not caring if she got a bite or not. Zach, in contrast, was fizzing with excitement; he squeaked when the Goggle Drops were dripped into his eyes, he gasped and cooed when he was told about the Glare and Gloam, and he whooped with joy when his line went taut and he hauled a wet, flapping trout into the boat.

'What a whopper!' Huffkin declared.

'Jolly good catch for a beginner,' said Humdudgeon.

'Hmm,' was the most effusive response that Athene could produce when Zach proudly showed her his fish.

Crouched in the very back of the canoe, Athene felt so miserable that she could quite easily have howled. For a few precious days, she had been allowed to share a marvellous secret, but now her brother had discovered it too. What was even worse, the Gloam seemed to actually *like* him.

The others were too occupied with baiting their hooks, watching for fish and sipping brew from a little leather flask, to notice that the weather was changing. Athene was the only one to see the storm clouds massing overhead, and the first of them to feel the raindrops landing in her hair. To start with, the big plump drops fell in dribs and drabs, but after a few minutes they pelted down like stones. If Zach had not been there, Athene would have been disappointed by the arrival of rain. As it was, she felt thankful. It meant that the interminable fishing expedition would have to be cut short.

With urgent strokes, the Gloam paddled to the nearest bank. Then, when they had all jumped ashore, they upturned the canoe and balanced it above their heads to shield themselves from the downpour. Humdudgeon thought that the rain might ease off, but he didn't turn out to be right. Eventually, they all agreed to abandon the night's activities and head for home.

'Want us to come with you?' said Huffkin.

'No, we'll be fine,' said Athene. She couldn't possibly summon up the effort to be pleasant to her brother for one more second and she didn't want her friends to see her lose her temper with him. They might make the mistake of thinking that she wasn't very nice.

Bidding a muted goodbye to the Gloam, Athene took Zach's hand and pulled him along the riverbank. Then she struck out across the fields, making for Freshwater Farmhouse. The rain did not let up. The raindrops slipped down her forehead, catching in her brows and lashes before dripping into her eyes. Together with her tears, which had been brought on by the disastrous nature of the night's events, the Goggle Drops were soon washed from her eyes. Within fifteen minutes, her vision had reverted to normal and she could barely see her own trainers in the dark. Even though Athene had no idea of where she was or in which direction she should be walking, she continued to drag her brother along at a breakneck pace.

Thunder rumbled and lightning streaked across the sky. Athene peered through her spikes of wet hair, hoping to glimpse a landmark that she recognised. Her wish was granted when her feet hit tarmac and she saw the hollow tree lit up by a fork of garish lightning.

In the split second that she saw its silhouette, the tree looked monstrous, with its grotesque trunk and its branches like tentacles. She pictured the Low Gloam living beneath its roots, forcing their slaves to obey their every command.

Athene felt her brother tugging at her hand. 'My pyjamas are wet-through, Eeny. Are we nearly there?' he said.

'Nearly,' Athene heard herself say, 'but I think we should look for somewhere to take shelter, at least until the thunderstorm has passed.'

'All right,' said her brother tiredly. 'Where?'

'How about that hollow tree?'

Zach let go of her hand and ran towards it eagerly. 'It's like a cave!' he said, his voice filled with wonder.

Athene stood back and watched him as he bent to peer inside the trunk. She didn't shout out. She didn't try to stop him. He slipped into the tree and disappeared.

After a few minutes, Athene inched closer. 'Zach?' she said.

There was no reply.

The rain drummed on the road and the thunder boomed.

She waited for a moment more; then turned away, thrilled and appalled by what she had just done.

Chapter five

The Tall Lady

The road brought Athene home. Rather than attempt to find her way across the fields, she had the presence of mind to follow the narrow country lane along which she had cycled the day before. The lane wound its way through woods and over bridges; up and down hills and past field after field of weather-beaten crops, which could be heard rustling softly in the dark.

It was very late and Athene's walk was a lonely one. A handful of times, she had to crouch in ditches or nip behind trees to elude passing motorists and, once, she only just avoided being caught in the beam of a bicycle lamp when a cyclist in a waterproof cape freewheeled soundlessly round a corner. She knew that if anyone happened to see her, trudging homeward in the pouring rain, they would be bound to stop and ask her what she thought she was doing. Athene did not wish to be bombarded with awkward questions. Even though she was drenched to the bone and desperately tired, she did everything she could to ensure that no one would offer her a lift.

She almost managed to make it back to the farmhouse without being challenged, but her luck ran out as she turned into the driveway. The patter of footsteps close by gave her a hint that she had been seen. Then a voice called out her name. She spun round and saw two pearly dots moving jerkily towards her.

'Who's that?' Athene said. She did not recognise the man's voice, but knew, of course, that he was a Gloam.

'It is I, Pucklepod,' replied the man, and she saw his shining eyes stop just short of where she stood.

'Oh, hello,' Athene said warily.

'I was told that you had set out for home more than an hour ago,' the Chief of the Humble Gloam said, edging nearer. He didn't seem quite as hostile as he had a couple of nights before. He sounded perplexed, more than any-thing. Athene felt the touch of his hand upon her arm and his voice took on a worried note. 'You look like a half-drowned rabbit. What's happened to you, Athene? And, tell me, where is your little brother, Zach?'

'My brother?' Athene said. Pucklepod's words were like a slap across her cheek.

'He was with you tonight, wasn't he?' Pucklepod said. 'I bumped into Huffkin and Humdudgeon on my way to the huge white house –'

'That's where I'm staying,' Athene mumbled. 'It's

called Freshwater Farm.'

'Is that so?' said the Chief. 'You're a fortunate girl. Its gardens are full of good things to eat. There are slugs aplenty at this time of year and I fancied some for my luncheon – but that's by the by. When I met Humdudgeon and Huffkin they told me all about your brother. I hear he caught a fine big fish before the rain-storm started.'

The long walk along the lane had given Athene ample time to dream up a story which would explain precisely what had happened to Zach. She wasn't going to tell anyone the whole truth. Tricking her brother into spending the rest of his life as a slave was not really something that she felt would be looked upon favourably. However, once he had vanished inside the hollow tree, Athene had found that she did not want to think about Zach at all. She had pushed him out of her mind altogether. On the arduous hike homeward, all that she had permitted herself to think about was a fluffy, warm towel and clean, dry sheets and a soft, feather pillow for her weary head.

Her silence seemed to make Pucklepod uneasy.

'Where is Zach?' asked the Chief again.

Athene floundered for a moment. Rather than invent an outrageous lie, she decided to bend the truth. 'I . . . I lost him,' she said.

'Lost?' said Pucklepod. 'In this belting, great thunderstorm? What a thing to happen! How worrying for you, Athene – but don't despair! I'll summon the others. We'll track him down in a flash.'

'No,' said Athene. 'I mean . . . you can't . . .'

The Chief wasn't listening to her. 'Hie!' she heard him yell. There was a flicker of movement in the darkness and Athene guessed that he was waving his arms in the air.

In no time at all, a whole host of Gloam had arrived. There was agitated chattering and the sound of short, sharp orders being given.

'You won't find him,' Athene said.

'Yes, we will, my dear,' said Humdudgeon's voice beside her. He was joined by Huffkin who assured her that they wouldn't leave a stone unturned in their search for Zach.

'You don't understand,' said Athene, struggling to make herself heard above the hubbub of the crowd. 'Zach's not missing. He's gone . . . for good. He said he wanted to shelter from the rain. I didn't realise where we were until it was too late. The tree looked like somewhere safe to Zach. He didn't know that there was any danger . . .'

Athene heard a sharp intake of breath, and felt Huffkin's woolly-haired head fall against her shoulder.

'Heavens!' said the distraught Gloam. 'Poor, sweet boy!'

'How awful. How horrible. How perfectly terribly dreadful,' announced Humdudgeon fitfully. Then he sought out his chief who called for order and delivered the news to the rest of the tribe.

'Bad tidings,' said Pucklepod. 'The Low Gloam have got the young fellow.'

There was a stupefied silence. Then the Humble Gloam began to wail and moan and murmur fearfully. Many of the Gloam gathered around Athene and told her how desperately sorry they were.

Athene was so touched by the Gloam's sympathetic response that she almost forgot that Zach's disappearance was entirely her own fault. Most of the Gloam had never even met him and yet they were mourning his loss as if he were a close friend or member of their family. A thought suddenly struck her.

'What am I going to tell my mum and dad?' she said. Athene visualised her anguished parents, a queue of police cars in the driveway of the farmhouse and the cancellation of her holiday. The possible consequences of her actions tumbled down on her like tiles falling from a rickety roof.

'We'll take care of it,' she heard Pucklepod say. 'Don't you worry, Athene. We'll take care of it all.'

After a restless night's sleep, Athene awoke. For about a second or two, her mind was a blank and then she remembered everything that had taken place a few hours before: the storm, her brother's departure and the long walk home. She might have dismissed it as a nightmare if she had not spied her wrinkled clothes in a damp heap on the carpet and her mud-spattered trainers lying next to them.

'It really did happen,' she said.

Athene got out of bed and opened her bedroom door. If it had been discovered that Zach was missing, she would have expected to hear shrill, panic-stricken voices and the endless ringing of telephones; but Athene heard nothing of the kind. The house was as quiet as a tomb.

Pucklepod had promised that the Gloam would fix everything. Perhaps his claim had not been over-confident. Even though Athene had been warned that escaping from the lair of the Low Gloam was nigh on impossible, she supposed that the Humble Gloam might have found a way to fetch her brother back. Athene couldn't help feeling disappointed at this thought.

Cautiously, she opened the door of her parents' room.

Light streamed in through the windows. No one was there. Her parents' bed had had its pillows straightened and the bedspread smoothed neatly over the mattress. Zach's camp bed was nowhere to be seen. Thinking that it could have been folded up and stowed somewhere,

Athene began to hunt around the room. She did not find the camp bed. Neither did she come across Zach's suitcase, his drawing pad or any of his toys. She opened the wardrobe and rifled through drawers. His clothes were missing too.

'How odd,' Athene said.

Without returning to her room to put on her slippers or her dressing gown, she ran downstairs. In the living room, she found her parents sitting at a table set for three.

'Morning, Athene!' said her dad warmly. He helped himself to a knob of butter and spread it on his toast. 'What do you fancy doing today? We could visit the caves at Wookey Hole or go shopping in Weston or climb to the top of Glastonbury Tor.'

'Aren't you hungry, darling?' said Athene's mum. 'Come and sit down. There's a wealth of choice this morning. Look, you could have stewed fruit and yoghurt or toast – or Ginnie will cook you up a fried breakfast if you want.'

'Mushrooms, bacon, sausages, eggs . . . the works,' said Athene's dad.

Athene didn't know what to say. She couldn't understand why her parents weren't beside themselves with worry about Zach. Far from being frantic and upset, they both seemed to be in the cheeriest of moods. Neither of them mentioned him or showed any interest in where he might be.

Athene sat down at the table, too puzzled to do anything but stare at a spoon.

Seconds later, Podge burst into the living room, wagging his tail and drooling slightly. A few paces behind him came Ginnie in an apron, carrying a large plate of steaming food in each hand.

'Nothing like a fry-up to start the day,' said Athene's dad, seizing his knife and fork in readiness.

'Would you like a cooked breakfast too?' Ginnie asked Athene. 'There's plenty of bacon – and the eggs were laid this morning.'

Athene did not answer. She had more important things to think about than what she was going to choose to eat. 'Why have you only set three places?' she asked. 'Won't . . . um . . . anyone else be joining us for breakfast?'

'Bless you, no,' said Ginnie. 'We don't eat with guests. Jonnie and I always have ours in the kitchen.'

Athene looked at her intently. 'So there aren't any other people staying here?' she said.

'No, sweetie. Just you and your mum and dad.'

The Humble Gloam had kept their promise. They had taken care of everything marvellously. To save Athene's parents from any distress they had cast a spell on everyone in the farmhouse. No one had realised that Zach had gone missing because they had been magically persuaded that he did not exist at all. The Gloam must have been very busy in the night. As well as performing magic (and, surely, it must have been a complicated spell), they had searched the house from top to bottom, removing every single item that belonged to Zach. They had even remembered to take away one place setting from the breakfast table and, somehow or other, they had sneaked into the Enrights' car, for when Athene climbed into the back seat she saw that Zach's story tapes were gone from the seat pocket and the window was no longer smeared with sticky fingerprints.

Athene found it weird at first. She had borne six gruelling, excruciating years of having her brother hanging around and spoiling her life and she couldn't really believe that he'd vanished from it. She half expected him to jump out from behind her and announce that he'd been playing a hiding game, but as the day wore on, Athene became more and more convinced that Zach was never going to reappear.

The weather wasn't perfect, but despite the drizzle and the overcast skies, it was a wonderful day. Having the undivided attention of both parents was a truly glorious feeling. They took her to the caves at Wookey Hole and then to the town of Weston-super-Mare where they walked arm in arm along the seafront and taught her to skim flat stones so that they bounced across the water. Then they browsed the shops and bought Athene a necklace made from haematite before stopping for tea and a slice of jam sponge at a cosy little café on the pier.

By the time that they returned to the farmhouse, Athene was feeling extremely happy, but her day of being entertained and cosseted was not over yet.

While her parents settled down to read in the living room, Athene was treated to a guided tour of the Stirrups' farmyard by Jonnie and Podge. She was introduced to the chickens and the small family of Aylesbury ducks; nibbled by the goats; encouraged to pat the flanks of Rachel, the Jersey cow; and allowed to lean into the pigsty where three Gloucester Old Spot pigs were guzzling their supper. Athene rubbed their smooth pink backs whilst Jonnie told her all about the night that they had run away. The pigs, whose names were Flute, Stout and Starveling, had managed to squeeze out of their sty and had all gone trotting off on an adventure. They had been discovered the next morning, in the garden of a Justice of the Peace who was most surprised to find three full-grown pigs rootling about in her flower beds.

A game of knockout whist was undertaken afterwards and Jonnie lit the log-burning stove in the living room because the evening had turned quite cold. When bedtime arrived, Athene climbed the stairs with a blissful smile on her face. The day had been lovely from beginning to end and she couldn't wait to record every detail in her diary.

She sat down on her bed and gave a contented sigh. Then she picked up her pen, reached for her diary and opened it.

The page for the seventh of August should have been blank, but it wasn't. Drawn clumsily in green felt tip was a picture of a tall, stick woman with mad, spidery hands and a very long dress. It was one of Zach's.

Athene was speechless with shock. She stared at the picture uncomprehendingly until her brain worked out how it could have got there. The day before, she had found a green pen lying on her bed. Its discovery had alerted her to the fact that Zach had been in her room – and now she knew exactly what he'd been doing with the pen.

In a fit of anger, Athene ripped out the page.

The Humble Gloam had done a thorough sweep of the house. They had endeavoured to get rid of every single thing that showed that Zach existed. They had done their utmost to remove every piece of evidence and yet they had not been scrupulous enough.

She screwed the page into a ball and flung it into a wastepaper basket.

Throwing it away didn't help. Although Athene could not see it any more, she knew that the drawing was still there in the room and she could not feel at ease until it was gone. She thought about disposing of it in the dustbin outside and then she had a better idea. There was a chance that the log-burning stove in the living room was still alight. She could drop the drawing amongst its embers where it would shrivel into ash; and ash would not be able to torment her.

Handling the screwed-up drawing as if it were a time bomb, she ran swiftly down the stairs and into the living room. No one was there except for Crumbs the cat, who was sitting on the arm of one of the easy chairs. Crumbs fixed Athene with a critical gaze as she hastened over to the stove.

'Stop staring at me, cat,' Athene said, opening the stove door.

She held the ball of paper tightly. It was the only remaining thing which could be identified as Zach's. Once she had got rid of it there would be nothing to show that she'd ever had a brother. Athene's fingers uncurled. The paper trembled on her palm. She urged herself to throw it in.

Chapter Six

Athene's Make-over

A thene closed the stove door with a clunk. She stayed where she was. Getting up from her kneeling position seemed to require too much effort. She felt out of breath – as if she'd just competed in a race. But it hadn't been a race, of course; it had been more like a test, the outcome of which would determine whether her next few days would be fun-filled and carefree or fraught with hardship and danger. Athene groaned. It dismayed her to feel so weak. She knew that she would need to summon all her strength from now on, in order to face the perils that lay ahead.

A nudge from the nose of Crumbs the cat interrupted Athene's thoughts. She ran one hand along the cat's soft, stripy back. She might have used her other hand to stroke Crumbs, too, had it not been clenched around Zach's drawing.

When Crumbs had tired of being caressed and had wandered away, Athene opened her hand and smoothed out the page from her diary. She took a long look at Zach's picture of the tall lady, which when it had come to the crunch, she had not been able to destroy.

Naively, she had imagined that she could forget about Zach and get on with her life without feeling the tiniest twinge of guilt, but in the last few minutes she had realised that blocking out your conscience wasn't easy.

She got up from the floor and with a heavy heart and a weary tread, Athene went upstairs to pack a bag. She knew what she would have to do.

Thinking that she'd need a torch to guide her to the Humble Gloam's encampment, Athene had put one in the pocket of her coat, but as it turned out, she did not need to use it. Huffkin and Humdudgeon were waiting for her in the usual place.

'It worked, did it? The spell?' said Huffkin. The two Gloam poked their heads around the trunk of the sycamore tree and looked expectantly at her.

'It did,' Athene said, smiling weakly at them both. 'Thanks. The spell was great. My mum and dad were clueless. They couldn't remember Zach at all. You must have gone to a lot of trouble. I'm grateful.'

'Taking a trip?' Humdudgeon said.

'Pardon?' said Athene.

'The bag,' Humdudgeon said, indicating the bulging rucksack which Athene had strapped to her back. 'Where are you bound?' he said glibly. 'Up a mountain?'

'I'm going down rather than up,' Athene responded darkly. 'Listen, I've got a favour to ask. I'd like some more of those Goggle Drops, if you can get them. I'll probably need a big bottleful.'

The two Gloam were dumbfounded. 'We might be able to get them for you by the end of the week,' ventured Huffkin in a puzzled voice.

'That won't do,' Athene said. 'I have to have them tonight.'

'Why?' Humdudgeon said. 'What for? What the devil's the matter, Athene? Are you planning to run away?'

'Not exactly,' she replied. 'I'm going to bring my brother back. I'm going down the hollow tree to where the Low Gloam live.'

Huffkin and Humdudgeon both gave a horrified gasp and clutched each other in fright.

As they walked across the fields to the place where the Humble Gloam gathered at night, Huffkin and Humdudgeon tried to talk her out of it, but Athene would not be dissuaded. She was just as adamant when Pucklepod and the rest of the Gloam begged her to reconsider.

'I've made up my mind to go. It's as simple as that,' she said.

'But no one joins the Low Gloam *voluntarily*,' said Pucklepod, struggling to comprehend why anyone would do such a thing. 'Once the Low Gloam have you in their clutches, they'll never let you go again. The same spell that pulls you underground keeps you confined there. It's like being in a cage that doesn't have a key. You can't escape. There's no way you'd manage it.'

The eighty-three-year-old woman called Dottle, whom Athene had met a few nights before, forged a path through the little crowd by rapping the Gloam on the ankles with her hazel walking stick to make them move aside. 'I say that if the girlie wants to go, she should,' she said.

Humdudgeon began to protest but the old woman shouted him down.

''Taint right what the Chief said, and you should know that more than most, young fellow m'lad,' remarked the old woman astutely.

'Oof!' said Humdudgeon as she poked him in the belly with her walking stick.

'Aren't you the youngster who found one of the Low Gloam's slaves wandering by herself in Moggy Wood?' said Dottle.

Humdudgeon nodded his head.

'And didn't you get into fisticuffs with two of those nasty critters when they turned up to recapture her?'

'Actually, there were three of them,' Humdudgeon

said. 'Great hulking fellows they were. Biceps the size of turnips.'

'That's as maybe,' snapped the old woman, squinting at him. 'The point is that the Low Gloam were seen above ground and a slave got free for a little while at least. The spell had to be broken for that to happen, didn't it? And if a thing can be done once, it can be done again.'

'She's right,' said Huffkin and the rest of the Humble Gloam murmured in reluctant agreement.

Dottle seized one of Athene's hands and squeezed it hard. 'I'd go with you, dearie, but I'm a wee bit long in the tooth for gallivanting about underground.'

The Chief of the Humble Gloam cleared his throat. He seemed a little ashamed of himself. The old woman had shown herself to be shrewd and spirited and he felt a cowardly chump by comparison. In an attempt to save face, he thought of a way in which the Gloam could be of some help to Athene. 'I have decided that we shall send one of our bravest Gloam to accompany this young Glare on her quest,' he said. 'I propose Humdudgeon. What do the rest of you say?'

Pucklepod's suggestion was greeted with stunned silence at first. Then the Humble Gloam found their voices. All of them declared Humdudgeon to be the perfect choice, being as he was the pluckiest and the worthiest Gloam of their number.

'Right you are. Humdudgeon it is!' said Pucklepod officiously.

Over the sound of loud hurrahs being made by the Humble tribe, who were undoubtedly relieved that they would not be going themselves, Athene heard Humdudgeon gulp.

'It would be an honour,' he said, giving her a stiff little bow. Athene thought she'd never seen him look more depressed.

'What about your leg?' hissed Huffkin to Humdudgeon. 'Who's going to bandage it for you when you're underground? And what happens if you need to make a quick getaway? You're far too brave for your own good. I can't let you go by yourself.'

'Nonsense. Of course you can,' Humdudgeon said.

They bickered about this issue for a while longer and then Huffkin stood on a tree trunk and spoke in a loud, clear voice. 'If Humdudgeon's going, then I am too,' she told her tribe determinedly.

This fresh announcement drew gasps from the crowd.

Athene was bowled over. 'I can't thank you enough,' she said to her two Gloam friends who had bravely consented to come with her on what would probably turn out to be the most hair-raising adventure of their lives. She gave them both a grateful hug. She'd been prepared to attempt her brother's rescue by herself, but she had to admit that the task seemed far less daunting with two friends accompanying her.

A collection was organised. The older members of the Humble tribe were encouraged to part with any Goggle Drops that they could spare. Huffkin stored them in a thin glass bottle, which appeared to be a bud vase with a cork in the top. In an act of martyrdom, Dottle donated all her Drops. She said that it didn't matter if she couldn't see for a few weeks – she'd feel her way with her walking stick and if anything seemed at all suspicious she'd give it a good whack.

'Take this, too,' insisted Dottle, pressing a metal ball into Athene's hands. 'It's magic. I made it myself – from a Glare thingy I found in a field.'

'What kind of "thingy" was it?' asked Athene curiously.

'You know – one of them what-d'you-call-its with pointy bits that twiddle round and round. A clock, I think it's called.'

'Great!' said Athene. 'Thanks a lot.' She wondered what was so magical about it. The metal ball, which had a strap attached to it, looked fairly harmless sitting in her hand and it certainly did not resemble a clock. Thinking that Dottle might be affronted if she asked her what it did, Athene decided to consult Humdudgeon or Huffkin later on.

'Best of luck, dearie,' said the old woman warmly.

'Now, about your parents . . .' said Pucklepod, drawing Athene to one side. 'I was thinking that we might have to cast another spell on them.'

'Yes, *please*,' Athene said gratefully. Before she had left the farmhouse, she had attempted to leave her parents a note to explain where she had gone, but had found it impossible to write one without mentioning the Gloam. No matter how cleverly she had tried to word her message, the magic spell preventing her from talking about the Gloam had drained all the ink from her pen. The anguish that her disappearance was likely to cause her mum and dad had been worrying Athene greatly. Pucklepod's willingness to recast the spell that had so effectively wiped the memory of Zach from her parents' minds was a huge relief to her.

In half an hour, Athene and the two Gloam were ready to go. Huffkin had crammed a parcel of food and a flask of brew into a satchel, together with the bottle of Goggle Drops. Humdudgeon's load comprised three rolled-up blankets, a bundle of clothes and a small set of tools.

They were preparing to say their farewells to the Humble tribe who had gathered in a circle around them, when Pucklepod dampened their spirits by asking them about their plan.

'Ah,' said Humdudgeon, his face falling. 'Yes, we'll need one of those.'

The three friends stared at each other in alarm. With so much else to think about (what to take and what to leave behind), they had completely forgotten to focus on the strategy that they would adopt once they had entered the Low Gloam's kingdom.

'You can't just waltz in there, grab Zach and run out again,' said Pucklepod, unhelpfully stating the obvious.

'Well, of course not,' said Athene, frowning at the Chief's insinuation that they thought it was going to be easy. 'The first thing we'll have to do is find my brother and then we'll need to work out how to break the spell,' she said. 'It'll be a cloak-and-dagger sort of operation. We'll need to creep about and hide and things. Oh, I'm sure we'll manage.'

She was most annoyed when the three Gloam shot her idea to pieces.

'You forget, my dear, that you're a Glare,' said Humdudgeon, spotting the flaw in Athene's plan immediately. 'Remember what happened when I introduced you to my tribe?'

'I was mobbed,' said Athene, her heart sinking. 'Oh, I see what you mean. I'll be like a celebrity down there. I won't be able to move for people following me about.'

'Not unless we give you a disguise,' said Huffkin, tugging the bundle of clothes from Humdudgeon's back. 'We'll turn you into a Gloam. You wouldn't pass as a Humble because you're a bit too tall. We'll tell them you're a Gargantuan. The Gargantuan tribe live in an old dried-up well in the woods a few miles east of here.

They're all about the same height as you.'

'So, I've got to get changed, have I?' said Athene, eyeing the pile of Gloam garments that Huffkin was sorting through. Between them, they selected an outfit which looked the right sort of size and Athene disappeared behind a large oak tree to effect her transformation. She took off her jeans, hooded top and trainers and replaced them with a pair of comfortable trousers, a cardigan and some soft leather shoes.

She emerged from behind the tree to murmurs of approval. Then she was persuaded to kneel on the ground while Huffkin dabbed at Athene's face with a paintbrush, making sweeping strokes and stippling her with spots. Every few seconds Huffkin dipped the brush into a pot which contained a dark, treacly mixture. It felt as cool as moisturiser on Athene's skin, but didn't smell nearly as pleasant.

'I'm giving you a Gloam's complexion,' explained Huffkin. She was taking her task very seriously. She kept stepping back and appraising her work, like an artist in front of her easel.

'What is that stuff you're using?' said Athene, wrinkling her nose.

'It's called Blend,' said Huffkin. 'We use it for all sorts. We painted our canoe with it. It's waterproof, you see. It won't come off in a hurry, not even if you scrub at it. I've also used Blend to glue a cracked dish together, and Humdudgeon's rather partial to a spoonful of Blend in his brew.'

'I see,' said Athene, wishing she hadn't asked.

When her face was done, Huffkin gave Athene's hands the same treatment and pulled down the sleeves of her cardigan as far as they would stretch to hide her unblemished arms.

'The plait will have to go,' said Huffkin briskly, removing Athene's hairband and letting her hair fall forward so that it covered her small Glare ears. 'There, that's better.'

Athene wished that she had brought a mirror with her so that she could see the results of the make-over for herself, but judging by the comments of those around her, she gathered that the disguise was a convincing one.

They shouldered their baggage and said goodbye to the Gloam that had surrounded them, before striding swiftly out of the clearing.

'We'll take turns to watch for your home-coming!' promised Pucklepod. 'There'll be someone posted by the hollow tree from dusk to dawn. Good luck!' he called after them, and they turned to see him gesticulating madly, like an overwrought parent waving his children off to school on their very first day.

Chapter Seven

A Stripy Stranger

For the first mile, Huffkin, Humdudgeon and Athene talked about ordinary, everyday things. Then the mood lightened and they started to tell each other jokes, laughing uproariously even though none were terribly funny. When they had covered half the distance to the hollow tree, they stopped to replenish Athene's Goggle Drops. She had had two dripped into her eyes in the Stirrups' front garden earlier that evening, but they were losing their effectiveness.

'They don't last long, do they?' said Athene, hoping that they had brought an adequate supply for the amount of time that they'd be spending underground. It wouldn't be much fun trapped in the bowels of the earth without them.

For the last mile-and-a-half they walked without speaking, each of them preoccupied with their own thoughts; and at a quarter past midnight, they reached their destination.

The moon seemed to hang like an apple from the topmost branch of the hollow tree, but other than that the tree had no adornments. It was leafless and barren, with a wide gash in its malformed trunk. They approached the tree with silent dread. Joining hands, they half stumbled into a ditch and up on to a bank. The tree towered over them. Its branches curled above their heads like the bowed legs of a giant spider. Athene felt the two Gloam waver and tightened her grip on their trembling hands.

'There's no turning back now,' she said, and with those words she bent herself double and ducked inside the gash in the cavernous trunk, pulling the others in after her.

The Low Gloam's spell worked instantly. Its power wrapped itself around their limbs and tugged them downwards. The earth opened up and they were sucked below. Instead of falling freely, Athene and the Gloam were handled by the tree's roots. They were grabbed and tossed roughly from one root to the next. Dishevelled and bruised and smeared with soil, they eventually landed on a solid dirt floor.

It was cold and damp underground and the pungent smell of moist earth was almost unbearable.

'What an undignified way to arrive,' said Humdudgeon, straightening his jacket and brushing crumbs of earth from his lap. 'Are you girls all right?'

'Yes,' said Huffkin dolefully, although she did not look it. Her hair was a tangled mess and she had lost a shoe.

'We should have brought plasters,' Athene said, examining a nasty graze on her arm.

'Plasters? What are plasters?' said Humdudgeon.

Rather shakily they got to their feet and began to take a look around. They seemed to have been deposited at the centre of a crossroads. Low-roofed tunnels stretched away from them in four directions and they began to discuss which one they should follow. Every few seconds, a shower of soil dropped on to their heads from above and, looking up, Athene saw the tree roots writhing as they set about repairing the walls of the shaft down which the three friends had plummeted.

'Let's choose this one,' suggested Athene, starting down the nearest tunnel. She had not enjoyed the sensation of being thrown around by scaly tree roots and she wanted to get out of their reach as quickly as she could.

'Right you are,' Humdudgeon said, gathering up his bundles and limping after her.

Huffkin gave her head a shake and small clods of earth flew out of her hair. 'Wait for me!' she said in a loud whisper. She was about to hurry after them when she spotted her missing shoe and hopped on one leg down the tunnel while she struggled to put it on.

The tunnel was like an oversized rabbit burrow. Its roof was high enough for the Gloam to pass under quite comfortably, but Athene found it necessary to stoop every now and then. The walls were plain and unremarkable at first, but then they noticed that, every so often, a flat white stone had been pressed into the earth at shoulder height. Each stone appeared to be a sort of Low Gloam lantern because it emitted a dim, steady light. It seemed that total darkness was not tolerable, even for a tribe who had lived beneath the ground for many years. The two Humble Gloam and Athene were glad of the discs of gentle light, for although they could see very well in the dark, out-and-out blackness might have caused them some problems.

They had not travelled very far when they heard a scuffling noise up ahead.

'The welcoming committee, no doubt,' said Humdudgeon grimly.

'Perhaps we should go back,' said Huffkin in a wary voice. 'There were three other tunnels to choose from. We could try one of those.'

Athene was reluctant to retreat. It had been her decision to set off down this tunnel and she wanted it to turn out to have been a good choice. 'If we're quiet, we could just take a peek,' she whispered. 'You never know, it could be Zach. We'd feel pretty stupid if we found we'd run away from the very person we've come to rescue.'

Humdudgeon and Huffkin nodded in agreement and they fell into single file. Pressing themselves against the earthen wall, they crept down the tunnel with caution, not knowing what to expect.

To their relief, they were spared a confrontation with anyone from the Low Gloam tribe. They found that there was nothing in the tunnel except for what appeared to be a grey furry bottom sticking out of a hole. When the bottom came towards them and a black-and-white striped head popped up from its other end, they realised that the creature was a badger. He was an adult boar with wide cheeks, short tough legs and a whiskery nose.

'Evening,' said the badger.

Having been greeted in a friendly way, the polite thing to do would have been to say hello back, but they were too astonished to say anything. None of them had met a talking animal before.

'Didn't expect me to speak, did you? Newcomers don't,' said the badger, padding round to face them. 'Well, you'd better get used to it. All animals can talk down here. It's the Low Gloam's doing. Makes it easier for the bossy so-and-sos to order us about if we speak their language.'

'What were you doing in that hole?' asked Athene, approaching the badger boldly.

'Digging,' said the badger in a weary voice. 'All I ever do is dig. Those ruddy Low Gloam never let up: "Dig this tunnel; dig that chamber." There's no variety.

Anyone would think that digging's all I'm good at. When I was Above . . .' The badger broke off from what he was saying to heave an impassioned sigh.

'Why don't you dig your way out of here?' said Huffkin.

'Now, why didn't I think of that!' said the badger savagely. 'Hmm . . . maybe it's got something to do with the spell that ties itself round your paws as soon as you get within a snout's length of the surface. Yes, that could be it.'

Huffkin looked embarrassed.

'Ruddy newcomers!' said the badger. He gave a loud grunt and began to turn his back on them.

'Excuse me, Mr Badger . . .' said Athene.

'The name is Shoveller. What do you want? I've got a lot of earth to shift,' he said impatiently. 'I haven't got time to stand around and chew the fat with you.'

'I'm sorry,' said Athene. 'I don't want to be a nuisance, but I wondered if you'd seen a little boy?'

Shoveller tilted his black-and-white striped head and gave Athene's question some thought. 'A boy, you say . . .'

'He would've arrived last night,' said Athene. 'His hair's light-coloured and kind of untidy and he was wearing pyjamas. He would've been soaking wet as well, because it had been raining.'

'Rain!' said the badger wistfully, taking a deep, shuddering breath. 'I remember that. There's nothing smells as scrumptious as rain. It makes a lovely noise too. Pitter-patter, pitter-patter . . .'

'Shoveller!' Humdudgeon clicked his fingers under the badger's nose to focus his attention. 'Do you recall seeing the boy or don't you?'

'Actually, I don't,' said the badger, sounding surprised. 'Bit odd that, 'cos I've been scrabbling about in these tunnels all week. Would've thought that I'd have bumped into the lad. Haven't heard that he's arrived neither, which is a mite peculiar. I could ask around, if you like. What tribe does he belong to?'

'He's not in a tribe,' Humdudgeon said. 'He's not a Gloam, you see. He's a Glare.'

Shoveller had parked his furry bottom on the dirt floor and was just gearing up to give himself a good long scratch. At Humdudgeon's words, he stopped dead and his fur fluffed up in shock.

'A Glare?' said Shoveller, his ear tufts standing up on end. He shot Humdudgeon a piercing look. 'Are you sure of your facts, chum? We've never had a Glare down here. Why, if a Glare turned up in these parts, I don't like to think what would happen. Be tied up and put under guard, I shouldn't doubt. There'd be one heck of a hoo-ha, that's for certain.'

'You mean the Glare aren't liked by the Low Gloam?' said Huffkin. 'Why?'

'Not liked?' said the badger, chuckling to himself. 'That's putting it mildly, that is. Let me spell it out for you – the Low Gloam hate the Glare and I mean *big* time. As for why . . . you'll find out soon enough. Now, if you've finished asking questions, I'll get back to my digging.'

Athene glanced at her two Gloam friends. They both looked worried.

'We should find Zach as soon as possible,' Humdudgeon said quietly. 'If the Low Gloam are as full of loathing as Shoveller says, there's no telling what they could have done to him.'

'Don't!' Athene said, biting her lip. She'd been trying not to imagine what it must have been like for her brother, flung down the shaft by the tree roots and left to wander blindly along the narrow tunnels without any idea of what was going on.

The badger paused to give them some advice before resuming the digging of his hole. 'If you're looking for a Glare down here, I'd keep a lid on it,' he said. 'If you so much as mention the Glare, the Low Gloam fly into a rage. Keep your head down and your eyes open. That's the way we badgers like to do things.'

'How many Low Gloam are there?' asked Humdudgeon, glancing about him nervously as if he were expecting a whole horde to burst through the tunnel walls. 'Could we avoid them? If we happened upon a hidey-hole in a nice, quiet spot . . .'

'Work-shy, are you?' said the badger scornfully. 'There's more than a hundred of the devils. It's no good trying to hide from them. They'll find you, wherever you hole up. The sooner you show your faces, the sooner you'll get some grub and a place of your own to snatch forty winks. Now, if you don't mind – I've got to get on. Mustn't be found shirking or they'll take away my privileges.'

The badger turned his back on them and shuffled into the hole, presenting them, once again, with a view of his furry bottom.

'Which way should we go?' Humdudgeon said to no one in particular. From somewhere close by they heard a mysterious buzzing noise, like an insect trapped inside a box, but before they could discover what it was, Shoveller's voice answered them from the depths of his hole.

'Just keep walking,' his muffled voice told them. 'You'll bump into a Low Gloam sooner rather than later.'

Chapter Eight

The Low Gloam at Last

'I wonder why the Low Gloam hate the Glare so much,' pondered Huffkin, squeezing Athene's palm tightly as they approached a bend in the tunnel. 'It's very unusual. I know we tend to avoid the Glare, but we've got nothing against them – and the Gloam are a peace-loving people. We don't wish others harm.'

'It's scary being hated,' said Athene, her stride getting slower with every step. The thought of meeting a Low Gloam face to face was giving her the most uncomfortable feeling in her stomach. She thanked her stars that she had been talked into donning a disguise. So far, her Gloam appearance had deceived a badger, but the real test was yet to come. 'Do you think my disguise will be good enough to fool a Low Gloam?' she asked.

They only had to walk a little further to find out.

'Who are you?' said a self-assured voice, and a pair of Gloam with buttoned-up greatcoats and broad, hairy feet marched smartly towards them down the middle of the tunnel. The Gloam who had spoken was an unprepossessing chap. His face was scarred and he was missing a few teeth. His friend had a face like a ferret with a weak chin, a pointed nose and beady eyes.

'These must be Low Gloam,' Humdudgeon muttered. 'I'll do the talking.'

'Isn't their skin awfully pale?' whispered Athene, excited by her first glimpse of members of the Low Gloam tribe. It was frightening, but also quite thrilling to finally meet some at last.

'Yes, and their stripes and spots are very faint,' said Huffkin softly, her lips almost brushing Athene's ear. 'No need for camouflage underground.'

'We're newcomers,' announced Humdudgeon. He kept his voice strong and steady and gave the Low Gloam a respectful nod.

'Fancy that! Three at once!' said the ferret-faced man, blowing out his cheeks and nudging the arm of his friend. 'That's a first, that is. We're having quite a week of it. I thought that the otter was a rare sort of trespasser . . . and now three Gloam have shown up together. It's unheard of, isn't it, Nark?'

'Not puny, either, are they, Rickit?' said Nark, sounding impressed. 'They'll make good workers, I reckon. We'll be rewarded well.' His gap-toothed smile vanished when he had finished talking to Rickit. With a stare that was expressionless he turned to Huffkin, Athene and

Humdudgeon who had dropped each other's hands and were trying their best not to show any fear.

'Come with us and don't dilly-dally,' Nark said abruptly. Then he set off down the tunnel with Rickit beside him. Before they did as they had been ordered, Athene gave the Humble Gloam the thumbs up and they grinned at her. It seemed as if her worries had been unfounded. Her disguise had fooled the Low Gloam completely.

They had only walked a short distance when they came to a fork in the tunnel. A fingerpost had been positioned at the spot where the tunnel divided. It gave them the option of taking the path which led 'To the Stints' or the path which would take them 'To the Snuggeries'. Rickit and Nark chose the left-hand tunnel and Athene and the Humble Gloam followed.

'I was hoping we'd be bound for the Snuggeries,' Humdudgeon said. 'Don't you think they sound rather nice? Seems that we're off to the Stints, though . . . whatever they are.'

'Look!' said Huffkin in a loud whisper. 'People up ahead!'

The further they ventured, the more Gloam they happened upon. Some Gloam were stripy and speckled like Humdudgeon and Huffkin; the men were clad in thin shirts and trousers that were patched at the knees and the women wore pinafores with drooping pockets and ragged hems. All looked as if they were hard at work. Some rushed to and fro with handcarts while others raked the soil floor or smoothed the earthen walls or polished the glowing stones with feather dusters. Wild creatures milled about with equal purpose. Most were small mammals like hedgehogs, rabbits and mice, but Athene also saw a grass snake and a fox with a package in his mouth. Concerned about stepping on the mice, which seemed to have a habit of darting around unpredictably, Athene was careful to watch where she was putting her feet.

There were several Low Gloam too. They were easy to tell apart from the other Gloam because of their chalky white complexions, their multiple layers of well-made clothes and the confident manner in which they strode along. Most of the men were dressed in great-coats identical to those of Rickit and Nark.

'Isn't everyone up a bit late?' Athene observed. Her watch told her that it was almost one o'clock in the morning. Then she remembered that she was living in Gloam time and that night was day and day was night.

Although no one stopped in their tracks to stare at them, Athene and the two Humble Gloam were aware that glances were being thrown in their direction. The looks that they received ranged from vaguely curious to sympathetic and downright sorrowful. It stood to reason that the girl whom Humdudgeon had tried to help escape must be underground somewhere, but he did not show that he recognised anyone and nor did any Gloam display a particular interest in him. A hedgehog was the only creature to speak to them. He muttered a hasty 'Hard luck!' as he rolled slowly past, collecting bits of leaf litter on his prickles.

Nark and Rickit led Athene and her friends past a right turn which would have led them 'To the Water Hole', and another right-hand turn 'To the Latrines' ('It's always handy to know where they are,' said Athene, making a mental note), and only a little further on, they arrived at the Stints.

'We bear left here,' said Nark, turning a corner.

The Stints proved to be an enormous U-shaped tunnel which had dozens of chambers dotted along it. None of the chambers had doors and so it was possible for Athene, Humdudgeon and Huffkin to see what was going on inside each one. It soon became clear to them that the Stints was a hive of industry. They passed kitchens where food was being prepared, carpenters' workshops where stacks of wood were being made into furniture, a place where rabbits queued up to take messages (rather like a taxi rank) and even a music room where someone was trying to strike up a tune on a zither.

They stopped outside a chamber which housed a solemn-faced Low Gloam woman who was seated behind a desk. Through its open entrance way, they could see her plainly. She was scribbling a list with a quill feather pen and every few seconds she had to stop to push aside strands of her long black hair which kept straying on to the paper. The woman was similar in age to Athene's mother, but she was dressed like an old lady in a high-necked blouse and a woollen shawl, with a large oval locket resting on her breastbone. She was concentrating hard and only looked up from her work when Rickit cleared his throat.

'Greetings, Tippitilda,' he said. 'We've got something here that might interest you.'

The Low Gloam woman set down her quill and stared at Athene and the two Humble Gloam as if she were looking at some wondrous miracle. 'Three?' she exclaimed. 'All at once? That's never happened before!'

'Out of the ordinary, isn't it?' Nark said, rubbing his hands, 'which is why we thought the payment would be quite a bit more than usual.'

'Six each,' said Tippitilda, reaching into a tin on her desk. She drew out a handful of small cubes which were toffee-like in appearance.

'What flavour?' asked Rickit, leaning forward and sniffing the contents of her outstretched palm.

'Mud and horseradish,' she replied.

Both Low Gloam seemed satisfied with her answer. They snatched the morsels from her hand, stuffed them in their mouths and took their leave without saying 'thank you' or 'goodbye'.

'Do come in and sit yourselves down,' said the woman briskly, indicating that Athene and the Gloam should sit on the chair in front of her desk. After a moment of confusion, Humdudgeon sat on the seat and Athene and Huffkin perched on its arms. In the meantime, the woman tidied away her unfinished list, opened the lid of her desk and retrieved a thick, leather-bound book which had a folded handkerchief as a bookmark. The book's cover made a soft thud on the desk as she opened it.

'Tell me what your names are and what tribes you are from,' she said, picking up her quill feather pen and dipping its nib in an inkwell. The leather-bound tome seemed to be some kind of record book.

'I'm Humdudgeon. I'm from the Humble tribe,' said Humdudgeon, making sure that Tippitilda spelt his name correctly. There were several column headings on the page. Underneath the one which said 'Character', Tippitilda wrote the word 'Fusspot'.

'And my name's Huffkin,' said Huffkin nervously, shifting to a more comfortable position on the arm of the chair. 'I'm Humble-born too. My grandmother was a Nimble so I can't claim to be *completely* Humble. I think there was also a Great-Great Uncle who was part Cantankerous.'

'No matter,' said Tippitilda lightly. She wrote Huffkin's name down and added 'Humble' next to it and then the word 'Truthful'. This made Huffkin blush guiltily, no doubt because she knew about the enormous lie which was coming next.

'And you are . . . ?' asked Tippitilda, raising her eyes to meet Athene's.

'Er . . . I'm from the Gargantuan tribe and my name's Athene.' Athene's words tumbled out in a rush.

'Is that so?' said the woman, and Athene watched as her name was entered below her friends' in the logbook. She was curious to see which word Tippitilda would choose to describe her, and was unnerved to see her write 'Overanxious'. The Low Gloam woman certainly seemed to be a good judge of character.

'Well, how super of you all to turn up,' remarked Tippitilda, beaming at them all.

Humdudgeon shot her a scathing look. 'You make it sound as if we just dropped in for a cup of brew!' he said. 'It was your tiresome spell that dragged us underground. We didn't come here on purpose.'

Huffkin's cheeks flushed an even darker shade.

'That brings me to my next question,' Tippitilda said. She glanced at another column heading in her book. 'How did you all come to be inside our hollow tree?' She smiled again, but this time it was strained as if she'd been upset by Humdudgeon's outburst.

Athene, Humdudgeon and Huffkin looked worriedly at each other. They hadn't thought that they would have to explain how they had come to stray into the Low Gloam's territory.

'Surely, you can't want to know an inconsequential thing like that? Does it really matter?' said Humdudgeon, acting as if the question were ridiculous.

'My columns must all be filled in,' said Tippitilda.

'We're tired. Couldn't we answer the rest of your questions later?' asked Athene, giving a genuine yawn. When Tippitilda shook her head, Athene protested. 'It's not fair. You haven't been so strict with everyone else. I can see lots of gaps in your book,' she said, pressing her finger on some spaces higher up the page. 'See, you've just put "otter" here and left the rest of the columns blank. How come you didn't make the otter answer all your questions?'

'He wasn't very talkative,' said Tippitilda. She sounded disappointed. 'I think he was in shock, poor thing. The animals often find the first few days rather trying. I make them drink a magic potion and it's quite a trauma for them to find that they can speak our language. Some of them take to it marvellously and you can't stop them wittering on, but others are horrified to hear themselves communicate in a human tongue . . .'

'Oh, I see. Yes . . .' murmured Athene, but she was not really listening. She had only bothered to mention the gaps in Tippitilda's book to buy herself more time to think. What reason could she give to explain how she,

Humdudgeon and Huffkin had trooped into the hollow tree? All the scenarios that she came up with were too far-fetched so she dismissed them. She glanced hopefully at her friends, but neither looked as if they were on the verge of thinking up a marvellous lie. To Athene's left, Humdudgeon was doing a fair impression of a fish gasping for air and to her right, Huffkin's expression was akin to that of a mouse who'd just been pinned to the ground by the paw of a merciless cat.

'We were on our way to visit some friends in Darlington,' blurted out Athene. (This wasn't a total lie. She had a penfriend in Darlington called Lucy Brown.)

'Is Darlington a long way away?' asked Tippitilda, stroking her chin with the topmost part of her quill feather pen.

Athene nodded. 'Miles and miles and miles,' she said.

'Then that would explain why you've got so much baggage,' Tippitilda pointed out, eyeing the bundles and bags which they had dumped on the floor of her chamber.

'That's right,' said Athene, relieved that Tippitilda seemed to trust her. 'And on the way,' Athene continued, 'we stopped to . . . um . . . to play a game.'

As luck would have it she chose that moment to put her hands in her cardigan pockets and, as soon as her fingers touched the object that Dottle had presented her with earlier in the evening, she knew what the rest of her story would be.

'It was a game of catch,' she said, 'and someone threw the ball too hard and it rolled into the tree. When we tried to find it . . . well, you can guess what happened next.' She took out the mysterious ball-shaped object and let Tippitilda handle it.

'How interesting,' the Low Gloam woman said, swinging the ball by its strap. She did not ask why there was a strap attached to the ball. She simply inserted 'Ball game' in the relevant column and left it at that.

There were lots more columns to fill, including ones headed 'Hobbies', 'Favourite Foods' and 'Disgusting Habits'. After Tippitilda had finished grilling Athene and the Humble Gloam, they made the mistake of beginning to relax, but their ordeal was not quite over. Offering them each a piece of paper, Tippitilda asked them to give her a sample of their handwriting.

'Whatever for?' Humdudgeon said in hoity-toity tones, but he bent to her will and scribbled down a few scrappily written words. Huffkin's writing was minuscule and neat, but, to Athene's delight, hers was the most admired.

'And now, I'd like to look inside your bags,' Tippitilda said, closing her logbook and putting it to one side. 'Lift them on to my desk and unfasten them, if you please.'

'What a liberty!' Humdudgeon complained, but he did as she had requested and in no time, they had heaped all their baggage on to the desk. Humdudgeon untied the blankets and loosened the cord of the bag containing his toolkit while Athene unbuckled her rucksack and Huffkin did the same with her satchel.

With painstaking thoroughness, Tippitilda examined the contents of each one, confiscating anything that she thought a captive should not have in their possession. Athene and the Gloam told lie after lie, describing the Goggle Drops as elderberry juice and Athene's torch as a sort of musical instrument. Tippitilda was completely taken in. She believed everything that they said, without seeming to have a clue that she was being fibbed to. In the end, she refused to let them keep Humdudgeon's trowel and a packet of crisps that Athene had brought with her, but to their immense relief, she let them hold on to everything else.

Swiftly they started to repack their bags and tie up their bundles, fearful that Tippitilda might change her mind. They had almost finished when Tippitilda appeared to think better of her decision. She held up her hand and frowned at them.

'Stop what you are doing!' she said.

Chapter Nine

Home Sweet Home

'Before you secure your belongings, I have something to give you,' Tippitilda informed them. She left her seat and walked to the back of her chamber where there was a large wooden cupboard. Opening its doors a little way, she rummaged in it furtively. Her behaviour was so secretive that Athene thought there must be something inside that she did not want anyone to see. *It's probably a higgledy-piggledy mess in there*, Athene thought. While Tippitilda's back was turned, Athene seized the opportunity to sneak round to the other side of the desk and have a good look for Zach's name in the logbook. To her disappointment, it was not there. The only other creatures that seemed to have been found in recent weeks were the stressed-out otter and a rat by the name of Ruffian who was apparently 'Headstrong and insolent'. Athene had just enough time to nip back to her place on the arm of the chair before Tippitilda returned to her desk, hugging three pillows.

'Here's one for each of you,' she said, dishing them out. 'As you already have blankets, I shan't issue any of those. Now, if you wouldn't mind waiting a moment, I'll sketch you a quick map. Be sure to memorise it well so that you can find your way around.' She took out a stick from her desk which had one end sharpened to a point and began to score lines in the dirt floor with it.

When Tippitilda had finished her map, Athene and the others stood up and studied it.

In the centre of the sketch was the shaft down which Athene and her friends had fallen and the four tunnels which stretched from it in opposite directions. Each tunnel divided into two and eventually joined a very long tunnel rather like a ring road which ran all the way around the Low Gloam colony and met itself. Clinging to the inside of this 'ring road' were four main settlements.

'The lower two are the Stints and the Squattings,' said Tippitilda, pointing at them with her stick, 'and the higher pair are the Digs and the Snuggeries. The Stints are where we are now and the Squattings are where you will be in a few hours' time. All the Gloam from Above mix with the creatures in the Squattings to eat and sleep and that sort of thing. The Digs and the Snuggeries are where we Low Gloam live.'

'What are those four tunnels at the corners?' asked Athene. It occurred to her that Tippitilda's map looked a little like a tortoise with its legs sticking out and its tail and head tucked in.

'This one on the top left is the Water Hole and you must already have passed the Latrines. Bottom right is the Coop . . .'

'The Coop? What's that?' said Huffkin.

'Not somewhere that you'd want to pay a visit,' Tippitilda said warningly. 'If you're a sensible Gloam and keep to our rules you'll never need to find out. Let's see . . . and up here,' said Tippitilda, striking the ground with the tip of her stick, 'is out of bounds without special permission. It leads to a place called the Sanctum which is where our chief resides.'

'So we're bunged in with the animals, are we?' Humdudgeon said, folding his arms huffily. 'I trust they've all been told about good manners. I don't want to be woken from my dreams by some creature slavering all over me or nibbling holes in my clothes.'

'You must get all sorts down here,' said Athene. 'I've seen lots of rabbits and mice and hedgehogs – and a fox as well.'

'We have two foxes living with us,' Tippitilda informed her. 'Their names are Fleet and Rusty. Both were in a bad way when they arrived. They'd run themselves into the ground quite literally, trying to get away from a murderous bunch of barbaric Glare. They'd been chased for miles, poor things.'

'It's a sport, supposedly,' Athene said, nodding. 'Some people hunt foxes because they think it's fun. My dad doesn't like those sort of people at all. He calls them toffee-nosed twits on horseback, but they're not seen in a bad light by everyone.'

'They're Glare, aren't they?' snapped Tippitilda. 'It's in their blood. All Glare are inherently bad.'

'Steady on,' Humdudgeon said. 'I don't think you've got your facts straight, madam. There are a few duffers amongst the Glare, it's true, but they're not quite as loathsome as you make out . . .'

'Our chief says they are,' insisted Tippitilda, getting rather flustered, 'and it's high treason to say otherwise, so you'd better keep your mouth shut if you know what's good for you.'

Her warning silenced Humdudgeon immediately, but Athene wasn't so easily put off. She knew that Shoveller the badger had advised her not to mention the Glare, but she wanted to be sure that Zach had not been discovered.

'You've never had a Glare down here, I don't suppose?' ventured Athene bravely.

'Glare?' said Tippitilda, tightening her grip on her stick. 'GLARE?' she said, brandishing it angrily. 'Down HERE? I should jolly well think not!' For a moment, it appeared as if the Low Gloam woman was about to lose her temper. Then she seemed to think better of making a scene, tucked her stick under her arm and pursed her lips tensely.

Athene dropped the subject. She had got her answer. The absence of her brother's name in the logbook had hinted at the possibility, but Tippitilda's reaction to her question had made it abundantly clear: Zach had not been found.

Tippitilda flapped her hands at them, manoeuvring them over to the desk where they were encouraged to pick up their things.

'You'll be assigned your duties tomorrow,' she told them curtly, 'but for today you can help the garment makers. Their workrooms are further up the tunnel to the right. Someone will collect you and take you to your quarters when you have finished your shift. Don't leave your pillows behind. Goodbye.'

'How rude!' declared Humdudgeon, when they had gathered up their belongings and traipsed back into the tunnel. 'She practically threw us out!'

'She got awfully tetchy when I asked about the Glare,' said Athene. 'I thought she was quite a sweet-natured person up until then.'

'Yes, I'm not sure that was very wise,' said Huffkin, keeping her voice low. 'Shoveller expressly told us not to talk about the Glare.'

'But I had to find out about Zach!' Athene said, not bothering to speak in a whisper. Huffkin put her finger to her lips, but Athene continued to babble away at the same volume. 'Thanks to my detective work,' she said, 'we know that Zach's name hasn't been entered in Tippitilda's book and we also know that she's never heard of a Glare being down here. That must mean that Zach's still free! He's bound to be wandering somewhere in these tunnels, hopelessly lost. If only we can find him before one of the beastly Low Gloam do . . .'

Athene was surprised to see the glum expressions on the faces of her friends. They did not seem convinced by her theory. Humdudgeon answered her questioning gaze. 'There is another explanation,' he said gravely.

'What's that?' said Athene.

'Look at the facts,' Humdudgeon told her. 'Zach doesn't seem to have been seen by anyone. It's as if he's vanished into thin air.'

'Yes,' agreed Athene, clueless as to what Humdudgeon was getting at.

'What are the chances of Zach evading capture?' Humdudgeon said scornfully. 'He's six years old; he doesn't know where he is or what danger he's in and, to cap it all, he can't even see in the dark!'

'Don't let's argue about this here,' said Huffkin, casting anxious glances left and right. 'We've been given orders. Let's hurry up and find these garment makers. We don't want to get into trouble.'

'We'll talk about this later,' promised Humdudgeon.

Athene nodded dismally, puzzled by the Humble Gloam's attitude. Why couldn't they share her optimism?

Every now and then they stopped to observe what was going on in the various chambers that they passed. They were on the lookout for clothing manufacturers.

'Look!' said Huffkin, tugging on Athene's sleeve. 'I can see someone with a pair of knitting needles. This must be the place. We'd better introduce ourselves.'

Huffkin ran up to the entrance to the nearest chamber. 'Hello!' she said brightly to a hunched old woman who was sitting on a stool with the beginnings of a sock in her lap. 'Tippitilda sent us,' explained Huffkin. 'She said that we should help you – just for tonight.'

They were not expecting to be split up. Athene watched numbly as Humdudgeon was taken to another chamber where darning and patching was being done. Huffkin remained with the knitters while Athene was led to the chamber next door which contained four spinning wheels. Her task was to tease apart lumps of raw wool before giving it to the spinners who turned it into yarn. She went about her job miserably, going over in her mind what Humdudgeon had said about Zach until her basket of raw wool was empty.

She cheered up briefly when she witnessed Gloam magic performed for the very first time. An old bow-legged Gloam with enormous crinkled ears held a single strand of wool between his forefinger and thumb. He dipped his other hand into a pouch attached to his belt and sprinkled a pinch of powder on the strand. Then he took a huge breath as if he were just about to dive underwater, sandwiched the scrap of wool between his palms and rubbed them with increasing fervour. At the same time he mumbled something that sounded like a whole lot of nonsense to Athene, but must have been a magic incantation because, in no time at all, great quantities of wool began to shoot out from between the tips of his fingers. When the old Gloam had finished repeating the magic spell, he wiped his hands on his trousers, gathered up the wool in his arms and put it in a basket, ready for Athene's attention.

Athene was not perceived to be a good worker. She tried hard to concentrate, but when she wasn't fretting about Zach, she had enormous trouble keeping awake. She could not conceal her relief when a rabbit turned up a little after four a.m. with Huffkin and Humdudgeon at his side. The rabbit had been instructed by Tippitilda to take them to their quarters in the Squattings.

As they stumbled tiredly through the Stints, trying to keep pace with the agile little rabbit, they passed Tippitilda who was still hard at work, sitting at her desk.

'Tut, tut. Working late again,' commented the rabbit. 'She'll wear herself out, she will.'

The rabbit turned left, then ignored two further left

turns as did dozens of creatures and captive Gloam who had also been working in the Stints.

'It's quite a crush, isn't it?' Humdudgeon observed.

They could not speak about Zach in front of their escort so they talked about their working day instead. Athene told the others about the magic spell that she had seen being performed.

'Could you do that?' Athene asked her friends as they turned down a long, straight tunnel with Low Gloam sentries loitering at its entrance like a group of ne'er-do-wells on a street corner. A signpost told them that they had reached the Squattings.

'Oh, yes, it's easy,' said Humdudgeon. 'It's a simple Multiplying Spell. I can do it with my eyes closed. I'll show you later, shall I?'

'I wouldn't try it if I were you,' said the rabbit, pausing to sit up on his hind legs and give Humdudgeon a horrified stare. 'No one's allowed to do magic without permission from Lodestar. She's the chief of the Low Gloam and her word is law.'

'May I ask if anyone's ever gone against her wishes?' Humdudgeon said to the rabbit. 'Surely, there must have been a daring soul who's tried to break the spell that keeps us all imprisoned here?'

'The Confining Spell?' said the rabbit, his ears standing erect and his nose twitching feverishly. 'I've not heard of anyone who's had a go. Lodestar is the only one who would know how to undo it. It's said she keeps the spell written down in a special book in the Sanctum, but it would be impossible for one of us to get our paws on it. The Sanctum is guarded day and night. As for anyone disobeying her – there are a few mad doddle-heads who've tried. Take Nibs, for instance. He was working in the laundry and attempted a Frothing Spell without asking first. Some traitor squealed on him and he hasn't been seen since.'

'What do you think has happened to him?' asked Huffkin.

'Taken to the Coop,' said the rabbit. 'Most likely.' He took several leaps up the tunnel and came to a stop by an uninhabited chamber.

'This Coop . . . it isn't a nice place, is it?' guessed Huffkin, hurrying after him.

'Most certainly not,' said the rabbit. 'Well, this is where I leave you. Have a nibble of supper and get some kip. I dare say you'll be sent for later on. Oh, and don't be tempted to go for a wander after you've heard the Honks.'

'The Honks?' said Humdudgeon. 'What on earth are they?'

'The first Honk tells you to get to the Squattings in double quick time and the second Honk signals the start of the Curfew. We're not allowed to leave the Squattings again until the evening comes. A third Honk is sounded to let us know when we're permitted to set off for work. The Low Gloam aren't bound by the same rules, of course. They can do as they please. Be seeing you!' said the rabbit; then, having completed his task, he bolted back down the tunnel to his burrow.

The chamber in the Squattings that they had been assigned was not as spacious or as finely furnished as they had hoped. Essentially, it was just a large hole with three mats, a bucket in one corner, a roughly hewn shelf and one tiny glowing stone set in the wall. The smell of earth was powerfully strong, which made them think that the hole must have been freshly dug especially for them. There were three dishes of some sort of gruel just inside the entrance. As with the chambers in the Stints, there was no door of any kind.

'Well, this is a fine kettle of fish,' said Humdudgeon, once they had all stepped into the hole and had a look around.

Athene didn't respond. Avoiding his gaze, she picked up a dish, sank down on to the nearest mat and spooned the cold gruel into her mouth. She was not in a talkative mood. After several hours of being able to mull things over in her head, she had a feeling that she knew exactly what the others were going to say and she wanted, more than anything, to close her ears to it.

'It seems to me that our little friend isn't down here at all,' said Humdudgeon, letting the rolled-up blankets and his toolkit drop to the floor.

'I'm rather afraid it looks that way,' Huffkin said resignedly. 'I vote we concentrate all our efforts into looking for that Gloam who you tried to rescue, Humdudgeon. She's the only one who can tell us how to get out of here.'

'I'd better start a calendar,' Humdudgeon said solemnly, scratching a short mark on the wall with a chisel. 'It wouldn't do to lose count of the nights. We may be here for quite some time.'

Athene laid her head on her pillow and decided to pretend to be asleep. She closed her eyes and, to her dismay, hot tears began to course down her cheeks. It was all too horrid for words. Ever since she had made up her mind to come after her brother she had thought of nothing but finding him. She had worried that the darkness might have frightened him, that he hadn't been given enough to eat or that the Low Gloam had mistreated him, but it had never occurred to her that she might be looking for him *in the wrong place*.

The facts were too substantial to ignore. Shoveller the badger had not come into contact with Zach or heard that he had appeared underground; no Low Gloam had found Zach and brought him to see Tippitilda so that she could record his arrival; and during the whole time that they had been underground they had not heard a whisper that a Glare had been captured, and surely given the scandalous nature of the news, it would have travelled like wildfire. There could be only one explanation. On that dark, stormy night in the lane, with the rain falling in torrents and only the occasional streak of lightning to help her to see, Athene must have made a dreadful mistake.

'He probably went around the trunk rather than inside it,' Athene heard Humdudgeon whisper as he unrolled their blankets. 'That boy's still above ground somewhere, you mark my words.'

'Poor little mite,' said Huffkin softly. 'No one will be looking for him. Pucklepod and the rest think he's down here with us and his parents have had all their memories of him magicked away.'

Athene stiffened as a blanket was thrown over her. 'It's a right to-do,' she heard Huffkin murmur. Then both Gloam let out an exclamation, startled by a loud honking noise which sounded like a car horn being squeezed. A few minutes later, the same harsh sound resonated again.

'The Curfew's begun,' Humdudgeon muttered. 'They've got a nerve, these Low Gloam, haven't they? How dare they keep us penned up in this louse-ridden tunnel while they swan around scot-free!'

Athene felt absolutely wretched. To have brought the two Gloam below ground to endure a life of servitude from which they may never escape was bad enough, but if it turned out that their sacrifice had all been for nothing, she thought that she would never forgive herself.

The Gloam's mutterings continued for a while until the sounds of gentle snores reached Athene's ears. She wished that she could nod off too, but with their plight and Zach's uncertain fate weighing on her mind, she doubted very much that she'd ever get to sleep.

Chapter Ten

All Work and No Play

Although she had been sure that she would not get a wink of sleep, Athene must have dropped off at some point, because she was in the middle of a dream when a thudding noise awoke her. Everything looked black when she opened her eyes, but after Athene had groped around for the bottle which Huffkin had put in her rucksack and shaken two Goggle Drops into her eyes, the maker of the sound was revealed to her. He was an earnest-looking rabbit and he was standing in the entrance of the hole, drumming on the floor with his long hind foot.

He was not the rabbit that had brought them to their quarters some hours before. This rabbit had much darker fur and a leaner build.

'Up you get!' he said, his nose twitching impatiently. 'The name's Coney. Rise and shine, sleepyheads! Time's a-wasting.' His ears made erratic swivelling movements as a loud honking noise cut through the air with the blaring quality of an alarm clock.

The noise seemed to jolt them into action. Realising that the Curfew had ended, Athene, Huffkin and Humdudgeon threw off their blankets, doused their faces in cold water from the bucket and ran their fingers through their hair. As they moved around their hole they grumbled about feeling stiff and sore. The floor had been a most uncomfortable surface to sleep on.

Coney seemed eager to be off. When they were ready, he dashed away at speed and they had to race down the tunnel to catch up with him. Training their eyes on the white underside of his tail which bobbed into view with every hop, they left the Squattings behind and started up one of the tunnels that led to the shaft. Here, Athene lagged behind. Although it seemed unlikely that Zach was underground, she still clung to the hope that she might glimpse his face amongst those of the Gloam. However, the rabbit was not prepared to wait for stragglers.

'Buck up at the back there!' he called, sitting upright on his haunches and seeking out Athene with a beady black eye.

Passing under the shaft was an unsettling experience. They saw the roots of the hollow tree hanging down like jungle vines and smelt a faint, delicious odour in the air. None of them could resist straining their necks in the hope that they might be able to glimpse a tiny patch of sky. To be so close to the upper world without any way of reaching it made them all feel horribly homesick.

'It's best not to linger,' said the rabbit. 'Just the scent of the place can make you break down and weep. A lot of folk won't even pass this way – even though it's the most direct route. It wrenches their hearts, poor devils.'

They left the shaft behind and continued along another of the central tunnels until they came to a T-junction and a fingerpost which pointed left to the Digs and right to the Snuggeries. The tunnel that they had arrived in was completely different to all the others that they had passed through and made them forget about their moment of misery when they had walked underneath the shaft.

'We're entering the Low Gloam sector,' Coney informed them. 'You'll find it's a bit more upmarket.'

'The floor is tiled!' exclaimed Huffkin, prancing on it excitedly.

'Never mind the floor – just look at the walls!' Athene said, her mouth hanging open in awe.

Gone were the bland expanses of earth and in their place were a number of intricate mosaics made from pebbles and scraps of broken pottery and glass. The mosaics covered both walls and, viewed from a few paces away, they were clearly a sequence of pictures, which seemed to represent a story. Examined up close, however, they looked like tens of thousands of little fragments all of which had been positioned with preciseness on the wall. Busily tending to one mosaic of a moonlit scene in an orchard with several Gloam collecting fruit in baskets was a small team of workers, consisting of two squirrels and a Gloam. They seemed to be removing every single piece of the mosaic and examining it. If the piece was cracked or chipped, they delved into a sack and replaced it with a fresh one, but if it seemed undamaged it was polished on a sleeve, or in the squirrels' case, their tails, and carefully put back in place.

'You will work here,' said the rabbit, bounding over to Huffkin and pressing a paw against her leg. 'As for you other two, your help is sought elsewhere.'

'I'll try to discover as much as I can about the Gloam that escaped,' promised Huffkin in a low voice. 'You'll do the same, won't you, Athene?'

'Of course,' Athene said, her face growing hot. Showing great self-restraint and good manners, neither of her friends had accused her of bringing them to the realm of the Low Gloam on a wild goose chase. It seemed to be an unspoken agreement that they should all abandon their search for Zach and concentrate on finding the runaway Gloam girl, who had made it above ground for a few brief hours before being recaptured and taken below again.

'You'll keep a lookout for her, won't you?' Huffkin whispered to Humdudgeon.

'Naturally, my dear,' he muttered, sounding mildly annoyed.

Bidding Huffkin farewell, Athene and Humdudgeon set off again, following Coney who was lolloping along at a slightly less energetic pace. Athene tried to study each mosaic as she passed it. One was of a building with a pitched roof, a huge door and no windows and another seemed to be depicting a battle of some sort. They filed past a number of Low Gloam who glided snootily by, casting disapproving looks at them, and a Gloam man from the Pernickety tribe who was slopping water over the tile floor with a mop. Athene and Humdudgeon stole a brief peek at the Digs, which were down a tunnel to their left. They saw a spotless floor with checked tiles, glowing stones arranged in patterns on the walls and lots of round, wooden doors with bell pulls and doorknobs. It seemed a grand sort of place to live compared with the Squattings.

Eventually, the tiled floor and the decorative walls came to an end and they turned down a path which sloped steeply downwards and was signposted 'To the Water Hole'. Athene noticed that the ground was scored with lines as if someone had been journeying back and forth on a bicycle. After a minute or two of walking downhill, the passage that they had been following opened into a low-ceilinged chamber with a floor of solid rock. In the chamber was a wooden cart similar to the handcarts that they had seen before, but with shafts jutting from it. Standing near to the cart were a gentle-faced vixen and a Scottish terrier with dark, shaggy fur, who looked extremely woebegone. Both were wearing harnesses. From the way that he jumped when Coney started to speak, it was plain that the terrier could not see well at all.

'The fox is Rusty and the dog's MacTavish,' said the rabbit to Athene and Humdudgeon. 'They're part of the team who deliver water to every home Below. A Horny-handed Gloam called Hobble used to help them but it's hard graft and he's getting too old for it.' The rabbit paused to nudge Humdudgeon with his nose. 'Humdudgeon, you will take Hobble's role. It will be your job to guide the cart and operate the brake, and you'll do all the heavy work too.'

'He means you're in charge of lifting and pouring,' said the vixen, running forward and wagging her long bushy tail. 'I'm so pleased to see you, Humdudgeon,' she said. 'It's been a struggle lately what with Hobble's bad back – and MacTavish here has been going through a rough patch. He gets awfully homesick, poor thing.'

Coney hopped up to the Scottish terrier and gave him a playful cuff with his paw. 'Cheer up, young fellow,' he said. 'It won't do any good moping. How about showing Humdudgeon what to do?'

'Why me?' said MacTavish, hanging his head dolefully.

'Go on, there's a dear,' said Rusty gently, giving his ear a tender lick.

Dragging his paws, the Scottish terrier padded over to the furthest wall of the chamber where, with the help of his nose, he found four wooden buckets and a coil of rope. 'You tie that on to the handle and drop it down the hole,' muttered MacTavish tonelessly.

'Ah, the Water Hole!' Humdudgeon said. He glanced around. 'Where is it exactly?'

They might have fallen down it if they hadn't been told where it was. The hole was just a little bigger than a manhole cover and when Athene and Humdudgeon peered into it, they saw the gleam of water and heard the rushing sound of a fast-flowing river, at least five metres below.

'I wonder if that's the river Axe,' Athene said. 'When my mum and dad and I went to see the caves at Wookey Hole, our guide told us that it ran for miles under-ground, fed by all the rainwater falling into chasms and things up on the Mendip Hills.'

'I know those hills!' said MacTavish, bounding for-ward. 'My owners, the Winstanleys, used to take me there at weekends. The smells and the sticks and the springy turf! We had such happy times . . . the like of which I'll never know again.' He lowered his head so that his nose brushed the ground and his tail drooped like a broken branch. Then he began to whimper. It was a pitiful, heart-rending sound that brought tears to Athene's eyes.

'I think you'd better go,' said Rusty gravely.

'Yes,' Coney said, butting Athene with his head and hopping towards the entrance. 'Come along, miss. That's enough chatter. We need to make tracks.'

'I'm sorry,' said Athene, patting the terrier carefully before she left the chamber. 'I shouldn't have talked about You Know Where. I didn't mean to make you sad.'

Leaving Humdudgeon, Rusty and MacTavish behind, Athene followed the rabbit back up the tunnel. On the way, Coney paused to wash behind his ears and they had to stop again and press themselves against the tunnel walls when the cart and its load rumbled past them up the steep slope, pulled by Rusty and MacTavish. Humdudgeon pushed the cart from behind, steadying the buckets every now and then and applying the brake when necessary. He was concentrating hard on his new duty, but raised his eyes to meet Athene's and smiled at her as he went past.

Having watched and waited while the rabbit found employment for her two Gloam friends, Athene was eager to discover what job Tippitilda had lined up for her and she hurried after Coney who had picked up speed again.

The rabbit led her along several tunnels and Athene followed, not realising quite where she was until they arrived at the shaft again. They did not try to get a tantalising glimpse of the upper world this time, but carried on through the dingy tunnels until they eventually rejoined the tiled passage with its glittering walls of mosaics. Instead of continuing along it, they halted in front of an archway which had 'The Sanctum' written in glowing stones above it. Athene was astounded when Coney hopped through the archway. She could not think why the rabbit would need to take her to the dwelling place of the Chief of the Low Gloam.

Ducking her head, Athene passed under the archway too. Then she trod in a cautious manner down a tunnel with a tessellated floor. On the walls either side of her were small, square mosaics of various Low Gloam, each of whom looked pompous, strait-laced and stern. Athene was instantly reminded of a set of equally alarming portraits which lined a corridor at her school, leading to her Headteacher's office.

'You're looking at all the Low Gloam chiefs through the ages,' said Coney, who was lolloping along at her heels.

Athene nodded. She had guessed as much.

At the very end of the passageway was a stout wooden door, studded with nails and flanked by two fearsome Low Gloam guards, both of whom were wielding sticks.

'What business do you have with our chief?' said the nearest guard.

Coney crouched in front of the guard and flattened his ears as if he were afraid of him.

'I was told to bring this newcomer to see her,' he said.

'There's a good bunny. Now scat,' said the guard, giving the rabbit a prod with his stick.

'You'll be all right,' said Coney to Athene, as she knelt down to check that he wasn't hurt. 'Just knock on the door. You're expected.' He gave her fingers an apologetic nibble, turned tail and raced off down the passageway.

Athene was sad to see him go. Annoyed with the guard for treating Coney so disrespectfully, she scowled and told him what a great big bully she thought he was.

The guard was astonished to be scolded by Athene, but instead of being angered by what she had said, he seemed to find it funny.

'You're a bolshie little madam, aren't you?' he said, when he had finished sniggering. 'I shan't give you a beating this time, seeing as you're new, but you'd better watch your Ps and Qs with Lodestar. If you displease her, she'll throw you in the Coop.'

'What exactly is the Coop?' Athene asked. The only kind of coop she had heard of was a wire mesh run where chickens were kept.

'The Coop is a jail where we lock up all the wrong-doers and mischief-makers and lazy good-for-nothings,' said the guard with a sickening grin.

'And is it where you put all the people who have tried to run away?' Athene said, thinking that she could have just discovered where Humdudgeon's girl might be.

'No one's ever been that stupid,' said the guard. 'It would be madness to try and escape, but you're right – if anyone did, they'd be slung in the Coop for the rest of their life, that's if the Chief was feeling merciful.'

Athene swallowed audibly. 'What's it like in the Coop?' she asked.

'You've heard of the lap of luxury?' said the other guard, smirking at the look of fear on Athene's face. 'Well, the Coop is about as far away from that as you can get. Imagine somewhere horrible and dank and foul where bugs crawl all over you while you sleep . . .'

Athene shuddered. 'I don't want to be put there,' she said.

'Well, you'd best be as good as gold, then, hadn't you?' said the first guard in an oily voice. Then he rapped with his stick on the door.

It was opened by a gaunt young woman who was dressed rather drably in a grey smock and clogs. She had thin, wispy hair that fell past her shoulders and the pale, clear skin of a Low Gloam. Her hooded eyes looked weary, but she was not too tired to grip Athene's hand and give it a hearty shake.

'Are you the scribe?' the woman asked.

Athene was stumped. She had not got a clue what

kind of work she'd been selected for. Should she nod or shake her head? – and if she did neither, would the Chief be furious and issue some awful punishment? Not that this frail young woman looked as if she would be capable of doing such a thing. From what the guards had told Athene, their chief was a formidable tyrant, but this mild-mannered, friendly Gloam did not appear to fit the bill.

'You *are* Athene, aren't you?' said the woman anxiously.

'Yes, that's right,' Athene said. 'Pleased to meet you, Lodestar, ma'am,' she said and dropped a curtsey.

No sooner had she spoken than the two guards burst out laughing, leaning upon each other weakly for support.

The woman laughed too, but not unkindly.

'Lodestar is my mistress,' she explained. 'I'm her servant, Dimpsy. Come in, won't you, Athene? I'd be obliged if you'd wipe your feet.'

Feeling rather foolish, Athene stepped over the threshold and found herself standing on a doormat. It was the first doormat that she had seen since arriving underground.

As she wandered further into the home of the Low Gloam Chief, Athene noticed other things which made her eyes bulge even more. There were rugs on the floors and pictures on the walls and proper wooden tables, chairs, sideboards, wardrobes and chests of drawers. It was almost like the interior of a real house, except that there were earthen walls where wallpaper should have been and there were no television sets or cookers or refrigerators or gadgets of any kind. Despite its out of date appearance and the lack of any windows, Athene thought that Lodestar's home was like a palace compared with the bare little hole she shared with Huffkin and Humdudgeon.

'This way,' said Dimpsy, leading Athene into a room which resembled a study. A ream of paper had been laid out on a desk alongside a quill and a bottle of dark ink. It occurred to Athene that they were the tools of a scribe.

'Sit down, please,' said Dimpsy, pointing to a chair behind the desk.

Athene did as she was told.

At the back of the room was a wooden trunk and, while Athene practised scratchy strokes with the quill feather pen, Dimpsy knelt beside the trunk and lifted out a book that was clearly in a shocking state of disrepair. The book was little more than an untidy bundle of torn and crumpled papers which had been tied up with string.

'This is our most precious tome,' said Dimpsy. Handling the book with the utmost care, she carried it over to the desk.

Athene sat bolt upright and her heart seemed to gallop in her chest. Could the work of literature in Dimpsy's hands be Lodestar's fabled Book of Spells?

'It's the history of our tribe,' said Dimpsy, dashing

Athene's hopes and causing her to slump listlessly in her chair. 'Over the years it has been rebound,' continued Dimpsy, 'but, alas, we can do nothing more to prevent its pages from falling into tatters. The time has come for a copy to be made. Lodestar would like you to write out the words from this old book on to those fresh sheets of paper. You'll make a good job of it, won't you? Lodestar's standards are very high.'

'Of course I will,' Athene assured her. For a moment she had thought that she might be able to discover how to break the Confining Spell, but having got over her disappointment, she found that she was quite looking forward to the task. Writing was one of her favourite activities and she felt that she was very fortunate to be given such a sedentary, undemanding job.

'Do you have everything that you need?' asked Dimpsy.

Athene glanced at the paper, pen, pot of ink and cup of brew that Dimpsy had placed upon the desk. 'I think so,' she said.

'Then I'll leave you to it,' said the Low Gloam woman, and walked out of the room.

Athene dipped her quill in the bottle of ink and started quickly, convinced that the assignment would prove to be a doddle, but it wasn't quite as easy as it sounded. It wasn't like a piece of schoolwork. You couldn't cross things out when you made a mistake and carry on writing.

If she made any kind of slip-up or spilled ink on a particular page, Athene had to cast that sheet aside and start again.

The first few pages were family trees, and without the aid of a ruler, Athene set about copying them. She was three-quarters of the way through writing out the sixteen children of Jibbinjak and Kristalina when a muffled explosion made Athene look up from her work.

'Dimpsy!' called a far-off voice. 'Come quickly!'

Athene laid down her quill feather pen and crossed the room. She stopped in the doorway of the study and looked this way and that. There was no sign of Dimpsy or the person who had yelled out her name. Wondering what could have caused the loud bang, Athene began to walk from room to room. Rather than finding the aftermath of an explosion, she discovered an acrid smell and decided to follow it. On entering what she supposed to be the drawing room, the smell became quite overpowering. It seemed at its strongest in the furthest corner where little squirls of smoke appeared to be seeping through the wall.

'DIMPSY!' hollered the voice again, only much louder and with greater insistence. 'COME HERE THIS INSTANT!'

The person was close by, of that Athene was sure. She hunted all round the room: under a chaise longue, inside a bureau, behind a dresser with a number of kitchen implements displayed on it. Finally, she gave up. There was no one there. Athene was just about to leave the room when she heard the voice again.

'FETCH A BRUSH AND DUSTPAN, RIGHT AWAY!' it said.

There was a soft crackling noise, and when Athene turned round, she almost keeled over in shock.

Where there had been a bare earth wall a moment ago, there was now a wooden door and peering round it, wreathed in coils of stinking smoke, was an old, sour-faced Low Gloam woman.

Chapter Eleven

An Audience with the Otter

'Who the devil are you?' demanded the old woman angrily, screwing up her almond-shaped eyes and giving Athene the sort of look that might well have caused her to run if she hadn't been frozen with fear.

'Nasty, pesky, prying girl!' said the old woman, batting smoke away from her face as she made her way into the room. 'Just you wait till I get my hands on you. I'll teach you to snoop about in my parlour! How did you worm your way into my house? Where's that wretched maidservant of mine? DIMPSY!'

'I'm afraid I don't know where Dimpsy is,' said Athene, finding her voice. From the woman's blunt manner and haughty stare, Athene felt sure that she had come face to face with Lodestar, the Chief of the Low Gloam. 'I didn't mean to be nosy,' she said, 'only I heard this loud bang and I thought I ought to investigate. I'm the scribe. My name is Athene. You asked me to write up your tribe's history.'

'Athene, eh?' said Lodestar, coming closer. 'And what type of Gloam are you? From your size I'd guess you were Gargantuan, but I've never seen one with such pathetically minuscule lugs. They barely protrude at all. Part Heedless, are you?'

'I am,' said Athene, shaking her head so that her hair fell more thickly over her ears. 'That's right,' she said. 'How clever you are!'

Lodestar clapped her hands together and gave a delighted cackle. 'I can't disagree with you there, girl. I have a brilliant mind.'

Buoyed up by the apparent ease with which she had passed herself off as a Gloam yet again, Athene looked boldly at the Chief. She was not in the first flush of youth and nor was she a great beauty, being plump and round-shouldered with her ash-white hair in a short, severe cut; but her eyes were mesmerising and Athene felt that they could only belong to someone with wit, intelligence and power.

'Ma'am, I'm sorry – I got here as quickly as I could,' came Dimpsy's voice, and she hurried into the room, an apron tied around her waist and her long, fair hair held back from her face in two girlish pigtails. 'I was doing the washing and then I heard you calling and I upset the bucket. There were suds all over the floor . . .'

'Don't bore me with your feeble excuses,' said

Lodestar scathingly. 'There's been a little incident and I need you to do some clearing up.'

Athene wondered what the Chief had been doing in the secret room. She guessed that the mess, which Dimpsy had been told to deal with, must have had something to do with the explosion. Smoke continued to billow through the half open door. As the smoke thinned, Athene glimpsed shelves filled with rows of jars and pots and bottles. It seemed as if the room might be some sort of larder or perhaps a kind of laboratory.

'I'll go and get my brush and dustpan right this minute,' Dimpsy said.

'Wait!' barked Lodestar. 'I hope you're not thinking of rushing off without taking this nosy parker with you. I caught her rifling through my things . . .'

'That's not true!' Athene protested.

'She was thinking of stealing my precious heirlooms, no doubt,' said Lodestar slyly. 'I don't want strangers wandering through my house wherever they please. Don't let it happen again, imbecile!'

Dimpsy appeared to be too mortified to speak. She grabbed Athene's hand and yanked her from the parlour, but not before Athene had glanced over her shoulder and seen the Chief re-enter the secret room. As soon as she had done so, the door vanished.

The more Athene read about the history of the Low Gloam tribe, the more she wondered why they had bothered to write any of it down. From what she had learned at school, history was all about interesting things like daring voyages across uncharted waters and battles and uprisings and outbreaks of deadly diseases, but according to Ploidy (the author of their history), the Low Gloam had always lived contentedly and without a whiff of trouble on the same square mile of land. Originally called the Lofty Gloam because of their propensity to live high up, the furthest they had travelled was a few hundred metres when the oak tree that they were living in was felled and they were forced to up sticks and find a new home in the rafters of a near-by barn. They had never fought amongst themselves or with another tribe and the closest they had got to being struck down by pestilence was when a Gloam called Bingle had given his friends a nasty cold in 1862. Lodestar had been the name of their first leader and his name was traditionally given to every Low Gloam chief (the most charismatic of whom was undoubtedly Lodestar the Ninth whose beard reached to his navel and who danced in the altogether under every harvest moon).

When Athene was told that she had done enough work and was dismissed, she heaved a sigh of relief. In her first stint as a scribe, she had copied out thirty-six pages detailing the first few hundred years of the Low Gloam's largely uneventful history, and she was more than ready to put down her pen. Her task had been so boring that she'd almost fallen asleep several times. Hoping that the dreariest chapters were behind her, because, after all, she had yet to learn why the Low Gloam hated the Glare so much (a spot of tree felling didn't really explain it) or why they had chosen to live underground, she passed through the front door of Lodestar's house and out into the tunnel where the two guards were crouched on the ground playing a game of dice.

'Mind your great clodhoppers!' said one, but otherwise they ignored her.

It took Athene a while to find her way back to the Squattings. The tunnels in the Low Gloam sector were easy enough to identify, but all the earthen tunnels looked very much alike and she lost her way several times. At long last she spotted the fingerpost which showed her the way to the Squattings and within minutes she came upon the clutch of half-a-dozen Low Gloam sentries who tended to linger by the tunnel entrance. Ignoring their snide remarks, she hurried into the Squattings, treading past holes of all shapes and sizes until she found the hole that she had come to think of as home.

Athene was accosted as soon as she set foot inside.

'What have you learned?' said Huffkin, seizing Athene's arm. The Humble Gloam's face was tense and hopeful.

'If you're asking me if I've found out anything about the runaway girl, then I'm sorry, but I've learned nothing,' said Athene. 'Well, nothing of much use.' She told Huffkin about what the guard had said; that, according to him, nobody had ever escaped or even been game enough to try.

'Everyone that I asked said the same,' Huffkin said dejectedly, letting go of Athene's arm. They both sat down on their mats and faced each other. 'It seems odd, doesn't it,' said Huffkin, 'that someone could make it to the surface and be brought back again without the others knowing.'

Athene agreed. 'I would've thought that news like that would travel fast down here,' she said. 'At school, last year, a group of boys climbed over the wall and legged it down the road when everyone else was in lessons. We all heard about it. Everyone knew who'd done it and what punishments they got.'

'Unless . . .' Huffkin said, deep in thought. 'Unless it was all kept a secret. I shouldn't think the Low Gloam would've wanted all their captives to hear about the girl's escape. It would have given them hope. They might have been tempted to try and find a way out for themselves.'

'So, it was all hushed up, you think?' Athene said.

They talked in this vein for a while, pausing every so often to pop their heads out of the hole to see if Humdudgeon was coming. A Nimble Gloam called Picktooth delivered their meal (three dishes of centipede stew and a plate of crumbly biscuits). Too famished to wait for Humdudgeon, they both tucked in. Athene was past being squeamish about what she put in her mouth though she wasn't best pleased when she found out that the little black bits in the biscuits were not raisins but ants. Still listening for the footfalls of Humdudgeon, the two friends told each other about their day.

Huffkin already knew quite a lot about the Low Gloam's history, having been working on the mosaics, which also told the story of the tribe's progress. Of the two mosaics that she had been restoring, the first was of the oak tree in its summer splendour and the second showed it lying on the ground with a severed trunk and the Low Gloam fleeing in the distance. Huffkin was quite amused to hear about the antics of Lodestar the Ninth, but what grabbed her interest most of all was Athene's account of her meeting with the present chief (whom they later discovered was Lodestar the Thirteenth).

'Smoke, you say – and a smell?' said Huffkin, rubbing her chin thoughtfully. 'And the door wasn't there and then it was . . .'

'And then it wasn't again,' Athene said. 'Do you think she was using magic?'

Huffkin was just about to answer when the first Honk sounded. A few minutes after the second short blast had rent the air, Humdudgeon showed up in the hole.

Athene and Huffkin looked at him with eager, shining eyes, but he did not even glance in their direction. He limped in without a word, went straight over to the bucket and dunked a cup in the water. He drank from it in noisy gulps; then sank down on to his mat, massaging his lame leg.

'Hard day?' asked Huffkin timidly, offering him his dish of stew.

Humdudgeon grunted. He wolfed down his meal and handed his dish back to her. 'I was late, wasn't I?' he said. 'Blast their confounded Curfew! Those ghastly Low Gloam have given me a punishment. On top of my other chores, I've got to clean out the latrines tomorrow.'

'How unfair,' said Huffkin. 'Er . . . I don't suppose you found the girl?' she asked him meekly.

'No,' Humdudgeon snapped.

'But you must have found out something useful,' said Athene earnestly.

'No,' he said again. 'Now, leave me alone, can't you?'

Humdudgeon pulled his blanket around his shoulders and turned his back on them.

Athene had never seen Humdudgeon in a mood. She found it quite upsetting.

'He's probably tired,' murmured Huffkin, 'and his leg's been troubling him. Those extra duties won't have helped to cheer him either. He'll be back to his old self in an hour or two, you wait and see.'

Their spirits low, Athene and Huffkin played a half-hearted game of noughts and crosses by drawing with their fingers in the dirt. Neither of them cared if they won or lost. When they had tired of it, they played I-Spy, but as there were only a few things in the room, that game did not last long. They felt that they couldn't really chat as it might make Humdudgeon even grumpier, and they couldn't whisper either because they had both been well brought up and they knew that whispering was rude.

A little later, when Shoveller the badger dropped by to see them, he was most surprised to find them sitting in total silence.

'Hello there!' he said, thrusting his stripy head through the entrance to their hole. 'What's with all the long faces? Didn't you like the grub? Centipede stew not to your taste, eh?'

Athene and Huffkin were immensely glad to see the hale and hearty, rumbustious badger. He was just the creature to cheer them up. They told him that the stew was satisfactory and asked him if he'd like to come in and sit down.

'Thank you kindly, ladies,' said the badger, 'but I can't stop, I'm afraid. Me and my mate, Fleet, are going foraging for worms. Thought I'd look in on you, though, as I was passing. Been wondering how you've been getting on.'

'We've been all right,' Athene said, trying to sound stoical.

''Course you have,' said Shoveller, nudging her with his nose. 'That's why you two looked so down in the dumps just now – and what's wrong with old sulky drawers?' Shoveller tossed his head in the direction of the blanketed lump in the corner which was Humdudgeon.

'We don't really know,' Huffkin confided.

'It'll be the underground life,' said the badger sagely. 'Even us burrowers get sick to the back teeth of it. It's tough to get used to feeling trapped all the time and some poor newcomers can't cope with it at all. It sends them right round the twist.'

Realising, perhaps, that he had been a little tactless, Shoveller tried to reassure them. 'But there, now,' he said, loudly enough for Humdudgeon to hear, 'that kind of thing wouldn't happen to level-headed folk like you.'

From the depths of Humdudgeon's blanket there came an angry sniff.

'Well, I must be off,' said Shoveller. 'I've got business to attend to.'

'Where are you going?' Athene asked him.

'Here, there and everywhere,' answered the badger, exposing his teeth in a rather disconcerting grin.

'You don't mean that you're going to leave the Squattings?' said Athene, astounded by the badger's nerve. 'What about the Curfew?'

'If you keep your nose clean, you get privileges,' the badger said with a note of pride in his voice. 'Has nobody told you that? Me and Fleet are allowed to leave the Squattings and go on a worm hunt once every fortnight. There are hundreds of worms hiding down here if you've got the wherewithal to sniff them out. That reminds me . . . did you find that boy you were looking for?'

Shamefacedly, Athene informed him that they hadn't.

'No sign, eh?' said the badger, with a sympathetic shake of his head. 'But you're still on the lookout? You haven't given up the search?'

'Actually, we have,' said Huffkin, 'yes.'

'What?' exclaimed Shoveller. 'Shame on you! We badgers are made of sterner stuff, it seems. You wouldn't catch one of my lot giving up so quickly.'

'We tried,' said Athene plaintively, 'but nobody seems to have seen him.'

'Is that so?' said Shoveller, his voice full of scorn. 'Did

you ask Midget the beetle? He may be half the size of my shortest claw, but he doesn't miss a trick. And what about the weasels, Gab and Blather? They're the biggest gossips down here. And I hope you had the sense to grill that otter. I heard that one was caught two nights ago and that's near enough when your boy arrived, isn't it?'

'Yes,' said Athene. 'But . . .'

'Goats butt,' said the badger sharply. 'The rest of us show a bit of ruddy backbone and get on with the job in hand.'

'Perhaps, I *should* keep looking,' said Athene. She had not yet been able to erase the possibility that Zach *had* taken shelter inside the tree and fallen down the shaft.

'I'll do it!' she said. 'I will!'

The badger had made her feel hopeful again.

'Good for you, Athene,' said Shoveller, and winked at her as he left.

Athene left the hole to find the creatures that Shoveller had named, but did so on her own. Her two Gloam friends had failed to be persuaded that the hunt for Zach was worth resuming. Neither of them had said as much (in fact Humdudgeon had said nothing at all), but Athene could tell that they believed that she was wasting her time.

The two weasels, Gab and Blather, were easy enough to track down. She found the long-bodied creatures curled up together in a messy hole in the Squattings. It was full of bones and twigs and animal hair. When Athene spoke their names, the tiny creatures lifted up their heads and slipped out of their hole with serpentine grace.

Athene knelt upon the ground and the weasels darted up to her. 'I'm sorry to interrupt your nap,' she said.

''S all right,' said one.

'What's up?' said the other, putting his paws on her knees.

'I've lost someone who's just arrived down here,' Athene said. 'A boy. He's young and pasty-faced. Shoveller thought you might know where he could be.'

'Like to help you, wouldn't we, Gab?' said the first weasel.

''Course,' said Gab, 'but we can't, can we, Blather? We haven't heard a whisper about a lad who looks like that.'

'Not even a rumour,' said Blather. They both shook their heads, then nipped back to their hole.

'Thanks anyway,' said Athene, getting up from the ground. She was disappointed, but not yet ready to give up. She still had two more creatures left to question.

Athene made her way along the Squattings, peeping into every hole. Some inhabitants smiled and waved at her, but others took objection to a stranger peering in at them and told her to clear off in no uncertain terms. Eventually she stumbled across Midget the beetle, inspecting his wing-casings under a stone.

'Hi, Midget,' she said, crouching down to speak to him.

'How do you do,' replied the beetle in a cut glass accent.

'May I ask you something?' she said humbly.

'By all means, young lady,' said the beetle. 'Ask away.'

'I've been trying to find a little boy,' said Athene. 'He's blind and weird-looking. His ears are really small and he hasn't got any marks on his skin. Have you seen a boy like that down here?'

'Regrettably not,' said the beetle.

Athene sighed. 'Well, thank you for your time,' she said.

'Not at all. It was my pleasure,' Midget said, waving a microscopic leg at her before retreating under his stone.

The otter proved to be a lot more difficult to find. After half an hour of scouring the Squattings, Athene was no closer to locating him. Many of those that she questioned, as she ducked in and out of the myriad of holes, seemed to have heard that an otter had arrived underground, but none of them could claim to have met him. Athene refused to curtail her search. The weasels and the beetle might not have seen her brother, but she felt that the otter would have had the best chance of bumping into Zach and it was important to seek him out. He was more or less her last hope.

Desperation made her bold. With as much confidence as she could muster, she marched up the tunnel and attempted to squeeze through the huddle of Low Gloam sentries who were patrolling the entrance to the Squattings.

They grouped together and blocked her path. 'Where do you think you're off to?' said one, smirking at her.

'I need to go to the Stints,' she said. 'It's urgent.'

The rest of the Low Gloam sniggered and surged forward like a rugby scrum, forcing her to take a few steps back. Athene glared at them defiantly. 'You'd better let me pass,' she said, 'or it will be the worse for you.'

'Hark at her,' said another of the Low Gloam, prodding her shoulder with his finger. 'Do you dare to think that you can threaten us? Go back to your hovel, pipsqueak. There's a curfew in case you hadn't noticed. You've got to stay in the Squattings until we say otherwise.'

'I must go to the Stints,' Athene said. 'I simply must. I've got to . . . er . . . get some ink. That's right. I need some ink. I've got Lodestar's permission. In fact, she's insisted that I go. I'm a scribe. I'm doing an important job for her, and if I go to work this evening without a new bottle of ink, she'll be really miffed. She'll hit the roof in fact . . . and when I tell her *why* I couldn't get some . . . gosh, I wouldn't want to be in your shoes.'

'But we don't wear any shoes,' said one Gloam

stupidly, wiggling his hairy toes.

'Shut up, Wenzil,' said another. 'I think we'd better let her pass. If our leader has ordered it then we should bow to her wishes.'

Athene could not believe her luck when the band of Low Gloam stood aside and allowed her to walk through. She held her head high as she strolled between them. Only when she had turned a corner, did she hide her face in her hands and allow her knees to tremble. Once she had pulled herself together she breathed in deeply and set out for the Stints to track down the one person who was bound to know where the otter could be found. She had heard that Tippitilda often worked late, but if the Low Gloam woman had gone home, Athene planned to go to the Digs and the Snuggeries and find her. Then she would ask her where the otter was.

Roaming outside the Squattings during the Curfew was a privilege that was rarely granted. She was bound to be stopped and questioned by any Low Gloam that she did not manage to avoid. However, Athene reckoned that if she kept calm and exuded enough confidence she would be able to convince them that she had permission to be where she was. If they saw through her deception she might receive a punishment, but she was prepared to take that risk. Finding her brother was all that mattered.

As if she were starting out on a crusade, Athene pounded down the tunnel.

She tired quickly and her lengthy strides had shrunk to dwarfish paces by the time that Athene reached the Stints. Every hole that she trudged past was empty. The cooking pots in the kitchens had been scrubbed clean and the wooden ladles had been hung up on their hooks. In another hole, newly-made furniture had been abandoned in a half-finished state and in the laundry room clothes had been pegged to washing lines and left to dry.

It was deathly quiet. The only sounds were the drip-drip-drip of water as it fell from the sopping clothes on to the ground and a gentle, rhythmic grunt coming from Tippitilda's office.

Athene neared the woman's chamber and felt elated when she glimpsed the desktop and saw a pair of stockinged legs splayed underneath it. Tippitilda was sitting at a curious angle in her chair with her head tilted back and her large antique locket askew on her chest. Gentle snores were escaping from between her parted lips.

'Tippitilda!' hissed Athene. 'Tippitilda, wake up, *please*!'

The snoring stopped first and then her nose twitched. Tippitilda's head rolled forward and finally she opened her eyes. She took a few seconds to recognise Athene and when she did, she smiled. 'Ah, it's Athene, isn't it?' she said, blinking dazedly. 'You're fortunate to have caught me. I was just about to wend my way home.'

Her dreamy smile faded as the last remnants of drowsiness left her. A look of tight-lipped disapproval appeared in its place.

'Suppose you tell me what you're doing here at this hour?' snapped Tippitilda, rising from her chair. 'I take it you have permission. Breaking the Curfew is a serious offence. Don't dither about in the tunnel, you foolish child! Somebody might see you. You'd better come in and explain yourself.'

Athene entered the chamber and sat down in a chair on the other side of Tippitilda's desk. She noticed that the Low Gloam woman looked dishevelled and exhausted. Her long black hair was dull and tangled and she had dark circles under her eyes.

'Well?' said Tippitilda, sitting down again. She rested her clasped hands on the desk in front of her. 'I'd be very interested to hear what you've got to say.'

Athene squirmed in her seat. Her courage failed her. She had convinced herself that Tippitilda was a kindly, approachable person underneath her bossy demeanour. She had thought that she could trust the Low Gloam woman, but what if she was wrong?

'I'm waiting,' said Tippitilda icily.

Athene decided to throw caution to the wind. She had taken risks and put herself in jeopardy so that she could find Tippitilda. It would be a waste of all that effort if she baulked now. 'I'm supposed to be fetching some ink,' she said. 'That's the story I told to get past the sentries, but the truth is that I'm looking for the otter and I thought you might know where I could find him.'

Tippitilda's mouth fell open. She seemed immensely shocked. 'Do you know how much trouble you're in?' she said. 'If I chose to report you, you would be severely punished. You'd probably be put on a diet of bedbugs and water for a week. What do you want with the otter?' she said, her outrage turning to curiosity.

'You deal with all the newcomers, don't you?' Athene said. 'All I want to do is ask the otter a question. I thought he'd be in the Squattings, but I've been hunting high and low and I can't find him anywhere.' She gave a heartfelt sigh, which was more self-controlled than screaming with frustration which is what she would have preferred to do. Athene had already failed to find her brother and the runaway Gloam girl and now she had been on a third fruitless search for an otter whose existence she was starting to doubt. What could have happened to them all?

'If you don't know where the otter is, perhaps I should ask your chief,' said Athene, beginning to lose heart. 'She might know what's become of him.'

'No!' said Tippitilda, almost falling off her chair. 'Don't do that,' she said, '*please*.' Athene could not have startled the woman so much if she had jabbed her with a pin. 'You mustn't speak to Lodestar,' said Tippitilda beeseechingly. 'Promise me you won't.'

'All right then, I won't,' said Athene, astonished and a little irked that Tippitilda had responded in such a panic-stricken way to a harmless throwaway comment. 'There's no need to get in a flap about it, Tippitilda. Do stop that awful whining.'

A mournful whimpering had started up. At first, Athene thought that Tippitilda was behind the noise, but when she glanced at the woman's face, she realised that she had quietened down. The woeful cries were being made by someone else. Athene got up from her chair and began to search around the room. She soon discovered that the noise was coming from the cupboard. Athene was thinking of opening the doors when Tippitilda jumped to her feet.

'He's woken up again,' she wailed, wringing her hands and pacing up and down the room. 'He's so very fretful at the moment. He won't talk; and he wouldn't eat a morsel until I offered him some of your strange, puffy, powdery food.'

'So that's why you took my packet of crisps,' said Athene. 'Could you tell me who you're talking about, because you've lost me totally.'

'The otter, of course,' said Tippitilda in an anguished sob. 'I've been keeping him in my cupboard. All he does is sniffle and shake. There's no work that he'd be able to do. He's utterly useless, you see, and if Lodestar found out about him, she'd be really unsympathetic. She can't abide wastrels and she won't stand for laziness. She'd throw him in the Coop, I'm sure of it – and, Athene, I'm awfully afraid that a week or two in that terrible place would be the end of him.'

'So, you've been looking after the otter?' said Athene, touched by the woman's kindness. 'Is that why you've been working late every night?'

Tippitilda nodded. 'I didn't want to leave him alone for very long. I thought that if I gave him some loving attention he might feel better, but he's hardly improved at all.'

'He's probably missing his home,' Athene told her. 'Otters live on riverbanks and in the sea and their diet isn't much like yours. They eat fish and crabs and things like that. I guess that's why he liked my crisps. They're prawn-flavoured,' she said.

'I'm sure you're right,' said Tippitilda, 'but I've come to the end of my tether. I just don't know what to do with him. I'd take him to my home in the Digs. He'd be happier there, I'm sure, but I'd never make it to my front door without somebody seeing us.'

'If I help you to smuggle him to the Digs, would you let me ask him my question?' said Athene cunningly.

To her delight, Tippitilda agreed. 'You may try,' said the woman, 'but you'll be very lucky if you get one word out of him.'

Athene did not intend to be overheard when she put her question to the otter. If Tippitilda discovered that a Glare boy was on the loose underground, she would be incensed. It was easy enough for Athene to persuade Tippitilda that the otter would be less anxious if he was questioned by one person rather than two.

'Don't make him cry, whatever you do,' urged Tippitilda worriedly.

'Cry?' Athene muttered as she leaned forward and prepared to pull open the heavy cupboard doors. 'The woman's got a screw loose, surely. Otters don't shed tears.'

As Athene yanked the doors open, her derisive snigger turned into a loud gasp and her hands flew straight to her mouth. The strength drained from her body and she fell to her knees, overwhelmed by the sight that met her eyes.

Huddled in one corner of the cupboard, wrapped up in a blanket with a ring of glowing stones placed protectively around him, was someone whom she had been longing to see; not the otter, but her little brother, Zach.

Chapter Twelve

Humdudgeon Confesses

He looked in bad shape. His hair, which was normally a bit of a mess, was so matted and grimy, that it seemed more like fur than human hair and his eyes were all puffy and bloodshot as if he had been crying for a very long time. Although it was comfortably warm in the cupboard, Zach was hunched with his knees against his chest, the way you might sit if you were bracing yourself against a bitter wind. The blanket that he clutched about his shoulders was too small to cover him completely, and beneath it, Athene could see his pyjamas which were encrusted with dirt.

She could see *him*, but it was more than obvious that he could not see *her*. Although his neck was straining in Athene's direction, his eyes were unable to settle on her face. With only the pitifully weak light from the cluster of glowing stones to make the darkness more bearable, Zach had no way of knowing that his sister had just opened the cupboard doors. Her reluctance to speak seemed to frighten him. He gave a little wail of fear and his chin began to tremble.

'Don't!' said Athene. One word was all that her tightening throat would allow her to utter. It was a horrendous shock to see her happy-go-lucky, high-spirited brother reduced to a cringing, miserable heap. It disturbed her to remember all the moments in the past when she had taken pleasure in seeing her brother disappointed or upset. She did not feel remotely cheerful now. In fact she felt nothing but shame and disgust.

And guilt. Immobilising guilt. It was her fault he was down here. It was all her fault.

The wretchedness that seized her turned to nausea and, for a moment, she thought that she might be sick. Then, quite suddenly, she felt all right again, and with this feeling of well-being came a bold determination and an air of calm.

She had done a despicable thing to Zach and she couldn't undo it, but she *could* try to put things right again. Whatever it took and however hard the struggle, she would see to it that he was safely spirited out of the Low Gloam's world.

'Zach,' said Athene. 'Don't be scared. It's me.'

'Eeny?' he answered. 'Eeny, is that really you?' Throwing off the blanket he crawled towards her, a smile lighting up his tear-streaked face.

Athene had held her brother in a headlock more than

once, but she had never given him a hug before. She leaned forward and, without any hesitation, drew him into her arms.

'It's going to be all right,' she told him, pressing her dry cheek against his teary one. 'Humdudgeon and Huffkin are down here as well and we're all going to work as hard as we can to find a way to escape from this place.'

'What's that?' said Tippitilda's enraged voice. 'Athene, what are you doing? What did you just say?'

The drama and excitement of finding her brother had caused Athene to forget to keep her voice sufficiently hushed. With angry strides, Tippitilda advanced on Athene and Zach. She threw the cupboard doors wide open and wrested the two children apart. 'Are you and this otter in cahoots?' she said.

'No, not exactly,' said Athene, refusing to let go of her brother's hand.

'I ought to take you straight to Lodestar,' threatened Tippitilda, glaring furiously at Athene. 'Didn't I just hear you plotting to escape? By rights, that kind of talk deserves the harshest kind of punishment.'

'You mean the Coop, don't you?' said Athene, her heart plummeting.

'Well . . . perhaps,' said Tippitilda edgily, distracted by the fresh surge of tears that were streaming down Zach's face. 'Must I attend to him again?' she complained, taking out a handkerchief and soaking up Zach's tears with it. 'I told you not to make him cry, didn't I? Otters are such emotional creatures.' Having wiped Zach's face, Tippitilda smoothed his hair and gave the weariest of sighs.

These gestures of kindness made up Athene's mind for her. Tippitilda might be a Low Gloam but she had demonstrated that she had a tender heart. Counting on the fact that Tippitilda would not want to cause Zach any more distress, she took a deep breath and admitted to the woman that she and Zach were brother and sister.

'You're an otter too?' said Tippitilda, not quite catching on.

'Of course I'm not an otter!' said Athene. 'I'm a *Glare*. We both are.'

Her confession came as a terrible shock to Tippitilda, who gasped and stumbled backwards. 'It's not true! You can't be Glare!' she said, steadying herself on her desk. 'What a wicked girl you are to tell such lies.'

'It's the truth!' said Athene. She squeezed her brother's hand. 'You tell her, Zach. You're not an otter are you?'

Zach shook his head.

Tippitilda shook her head, too, several times and rather more violently. 'No, no, no!' she said. 'You're talking utter nonsense. Glare are enormous, ugly monsters with jagged teeth and nasty staring eyes and if you're stupid enough to stumble into one, it'll make a terrible screeching noise, which will be the last sound you'll ever hear because right after that it will strike you dead.'

'I've never heard such a load of old hooey,' Athene said with disdain. 'Glare aren't like that at all! Who told you that rubbish about us? It's really quite hurtful to be thought of in that way. We *are* Glare, truly, but we're not horrid; we're nice.'

Tippitilda eyed them suspiciously. 'You're telling fibs,' she said.

'Look,' said Athene, her patience wearing thin, 'I can understand that you might have trouble believing that I'm a Glare – after all my Gloam disguise is pretty good – but how can you possibly think that my brother is an otter? Isn't it obvious that he's a little boy?'

Tippitilda looked uncomfortable. 'It was Rickit and Nark who found him. They were the ones who said he was an otter, but I wasn't totally sure. I'd never seen anything like him in my life – and he wouldn't give me a single hint. Just cried and cried and refused to speak. We've heard talk of the sorts of creatures that live Above. I thought he might be a polecat, but Rickit and Nark reckoned that they knew best. They said he must be an animal that lived in water because of his wet fur.'

'His fur?' said Athene in a puzzled voice. 'I think you mean his hair.'

'I *mean* his *fur*,' said Tippitilda, frowning. 'What else would you call that thick pelt?'

Athene looked at her brother. The only parts of him that weren't covered up by clothes were his face, his hands and feet and none of these were especially hairy. Athene was stumped for a moment or two until she realised the cause of the confusion.

'Oh, you are funny!' she said, attempting to stifle her laughter. 'You must mean Zach's pyjamas. I suppose they do feel sort of furry. They're made from a soft material. It's called flannelette.'

'Pyjamas?' Tippitilda said with a frown. It was obvious that she did not possess a pair herself. 'I see. He's not an otter, then,' she said. 'Nark and Rickit were wrong.'

'Completely and utterly,' Athene said, 'but it's an easy mistake to make, if you've never seen an otter face to face, I suppose.' This was a generous thing for Athene to say seeing as she knew quite well that otters and boys bore no resemblance to each other whatsoever. 'You know what, Tippitilda,' she went on, feeling rather sorry for the clueless Low Gloam woman, 'if you lived Above you'd meet otters and lots of other animals besides: deer with big horns called antlers and huge, lumbering cows and pigs with turned-up snouts and funny, curly tails and black-faced sheep and shaggy-haired goats – and more birds and insects than you could imagine. There are hundreds of wonderful creatures Above. It's such an awful shame that you're stuck underground.'

'On the contrary,' said Tippitilda, 'it is a privilege to live Below.' She spoke in a strange, dull way as if she were repeating something that had been learned by heart. 'We are fortunate Gloam. We are protected from all the perils and hazards that plague the upper world. Below is happiness and harmony. Above is devastation and disaster.'

'Who told you that?' Athene said with a disrespectful snort.

'Lodestar, of course,' answered Tippitilda.

'Oh, *her*,' said Athene, sneering up her nose. 'She acts like a great big know-it-all. I take it she's the one who fed you all that rubbish about the Glare? Poisonous old witch! I've got a good mind to tell her how completely deluded she is . . .'

'No!' Tippitilda said. 'You don't understand. Our present chief is not the one who introduced us to those ideals. It is the teachings of Lodestar the Ninth that we adhere to.'

'Lodestar the Ninth?' said Athene. 'Wasn't he that crazy, bearded guy who danced around in the nude?'

Tippitilda clicked her tongue against her teeth. She did not seem to approve of Athene's irreverent description of her tribe's long-dead chief, but nevertheless she nodded.

'How disappointing,' Athene said with genuine regret.

'I thought he sounded kind of fun.'

'It was Lodestar the Ninth who fought off an attack by the Glare at the Battle of Barnyard Bedlam almost a hundred years ago,' Tippitilda told her.

'The Battle of what?' said Athene, trying not to laugh. 'I've certainly never heard of it! Are you sure it really happened?'

'Of course!' Tippitilda said, sounding hurt. 'The Glare used terrible weapons against us. Our chief has a collection of them in the Sanctum. I'm sure she'll show you them if you ask her nicely.'

'I don't think she will,' said Athene, biting her lip. 'Lodestar and I didn't exactly hit it off when we met today.'

'Then, if you don't believe me, take a look at this,' urged Tippitilda, unfastening the old, oval locket from around her neck. 'This is a trophy from the battle. My great-great-grandfather, Ragabash, seized it from one of the Glare's most fearsome warriors.'

'Let's see,' said Athene, snatching the locket eagerly.

She slid her thumbnail into the slender groove of the locket and, with a good deal of effort, prised it open. Inside the case were two photographic portraits, bleached with age. At first, she believed that they were of the same young woman for the faces in both pictures had identical bucked teeth and widely spaced eyes. Then Athene noticed that one of them had a nose that was a little more crooked than the other's. It seemed as though they were two different women who shared very similar features. They were too close in age to be mother and daughter and Athene made up her mind that they must be cousins or – more than likely – sisters.

'I didn't know you could open it up,' said Tippitilda in astonishment. She peered over Athene's shoulder at the photographs of the women. 'Ugh! Repellent, aren't they?' she said.

'I wouldn't go that far,' said Athene, 'though they're not exactly beautiful, it's true. They're probably relations of the Glare warrior. He must have loved them very much to wear their pictures around his neck.' She scrutinised the photographs. The women looked no older than twenty-five and their hair was piled upon their heads in a very old-fashioned style. Athene looked at their pictures for a long moment. 'It's weird,' she said, 'but I can't help feeling that I've seen them somewhere before.'

'I don't think that's likely,' said Tippitilda, taking back the locket and re-fastening it around her neck.

Although Athene did her best, she could not quite persuade Tippitilda that life Above was a more attractive prospect than life Below. However, the Low Gloam woman did seem to come around to the idea that Zach and Athene might possibly belong to a breed of Glare that was smaller, better-looking and much more friendly than the Glare that her tribe had encountered in the past. They both agreed that no one else should be told that Athene and her brother were Glare, because it would cause aggravation and it might also result in a long stretch in the Coop for all three of them (Tippitilda was bound to get punished as well because she had harboured a Glare). On the subject of where Zach would be safest, Tippitilda was in favour of keeping him with her in her house in the Digs, well away from prying eyes. She suggested that Athene should come to the Stints in the early evening with a handcart. When no one was looking they would stow Zach inside it and wheel him to Tippitilda's home.

'What stopped you from doing that before?' said Athene, with an arm around her brother who had fallen asleep against her shoulder. 'I can't really understand why you've kept him in a cupboard all this time.'

'I wouldn't have got very far,' said Tippitilda. 'I'm a Low Gloam of high repute and we simply don't do manual labour. If I'd been seen pushing a handcart, I would have been stopped and questioned, and the otter . . . I mean . . . your brother . . . would have been discovered straight away.'

'Oh,' said Athene less brazenly. 'I see.'

At first, Athene was reluctant to go along with Tippitilda's plan. She did not want to let her brother out of her sight and Zach seemed just as unwilling to be separated from Athene. However, in the end, she was forced to concede that Zach would be far more comfortable and a lot more secure in the Digs than he would be in the poky little hole where she lived.

Explaining the situation to him was not an easy task. Zach got quite panicky and clung to her so tightly that she doubted whether she and Tippitilda would be strong enough to loosen his grip. He seemed to get a good deal calmer after she had popped two Goggle Drops into his eyes and poured a share of her Drops into one of Tippitilda's empty ink bottles for Zach to keep. She told him that she would see him in a few hours' time and promised faithfully to come and visit him every single day. Finally, with Tippitilda's help, she gave her brother a much needed wash, using buckets of water from the laundry room and afterwards they took a pair of trousers and a pullover from a sweet-smelling pile of freshly laundered clothes and dressed him like a Gloam.

Athene waited until Zach had fallen asleep again before she left. It made her smile to see her brother curled up peacefully in a nest of pillows in the cupboard, his hair clean and shiny and his face tear-free. She and Tippitilda tiptoed from the chamber and talked for a few minutes in the tunnel outside. Despite their differing outlooks they were starting to warm to each other.

'I'll see you this evening!' said Athene, and spread her hand over her mouth to smother a mighty yawn.

'Don't forget your ink for Lodestar!' Tippitilda reminded her. She produced a bottle of ink from her desk and pressed it into Athene's hand.

Of the few Low Gloam who were still awake and alert enough to notice Athene passing by, none guessed that she was nearly dead on her feet. 'I'm on an errand for Lodestar,' she said in a voice that warned them not to try to stop her. 'Tippitilda will vouch for me,' she told them as she scurried by. 'Ask her if you like.' It was the excitement of finding Zach that gave Athene the energy to rush home at such an impressive speed. She could not wait to share her tremendous news with Huffkin and Humdudgeon.

Athene approached the Low Gloam sentries who had let her leave the Squattings and flaunted her bottle of ink at them. The sentries accused Athene of taking far longer than necessary to carry out such a simple task, but contented themselves with calling her an idler and a slowcoach and did not dish out any punishment. Shrugging off their insults, Athene entered the Squattings and arrived at her hole within a few minutes. She expected to find her friends fast asleep, but when she stepped into the tiny chamber, she discovered Huffkin, sitting despairingly on her own, with her curly-haired head in her hands.

'You'll never guess what's happened!' said Athene, far too full of her own glad tidings to take in the fact that something was wrong. 'I've found him! Isn't it wonderful? My brother! Down here after all! It was a stroke of luck, really. I didn't know that he was there – in the Stints. Tippitilda's been taking care of him all this time and we never suspected a thing. It's mad, isn't it? Can you believe she thought he was an otter? They're a barmy lot these Low Gloam, aren't they? Oh, I'm so relieved, aren't you?'

Grinning widely, Athene stooped to shake Huffkin's shoulders and to push the Gloam's hands away from her face.

'Gosh!' said Athene, her smile disappearing. 'Not you as well, Huffkin! What on earth are you crying for? Things are looking up! Didn't you hear what I just said?'

'Doesn't matter,' said Huffkin in between a few gulps and sniffs. 'It's no good. It's all no good.'

'What isn't any good? You're not making a scrap of sense!' Athene didn't mean to be impatient with her friend, but she had been so looking forward to telling the two Gloam about her brother, Zach. To be greeted by such glumness and indifference was a major disappointment.

'He lied!' wailed Huffkin, clutching Athene and staring at her with wild-eyed anguish. 'He made it up. All of it – and we'll never get out of here. NEVER!' The rest of her outpouring of woe was lost in a series of hiccups and intensive, non-stop sobbing.

'Good grief!' said Athene, patting her hysterical friend on the back. She hadn't expected to have to comfort two overwrought people in the same evening.

'Where's Humdudgeon?' said Athene gently. 'Did you two have an argument?'

'He stormed off – and good riddance,' answered Huffkin bitterly. 'I never want to see him again!'

Athene was desperate to find out what had happened between the two Gloam while she had been absent. She was tempted to go in search of Humdudgeon, but didn't feel she could leave poor Huffkin in such a frenzied state. Fortunately, Coney the rabbit provided the answer by poking his inquisitive nose inside their hole and asking in a sleepy voice what all the commotion was about.

'It's Huffkin. She's upset,' Athene told the rabbit. 'I don't suppose you'd be kind enough to look after her, would you? I've got to nip out for a bit. I shan't be very long.'

Without giving Coney a chance to refuse her request, Athene hugged Huffkin and, getting wearily to her feet, she set off to find Humdudgeon.

He had not gone far. She heard him muttering to himself moments before she found him. He had hidden himself away in a roughly dug, deserted hole, which was barely big enough to contain an adult badger. Somehow or other, Humdudgeon had squashed his body inside. He had folded himself up as neatly as a deckchair with his knees pressing against his chin and his hands clasping his ankles. Athene couldn't tell, at first, whether he looked downcast because he was feeling sad or just uncomfortable.

'Hello, Humdudgeon!' Athene said, crouching down and beaming at him.

He turned his face away from her (with difficulty, for there was very little room in which to move).

'What are you doing in there?' Athene said, trying to keep her voice light and cheerful. 'Isn't it awfully painful to sit scrunched up like that? You're more squished than a sardine!'

'Mind your own business,' Humdudgeon said rudely, still refusing to look at her. 'Now, go away, please. I want to be left alone.'

It was the touch of her hand that caused him to break down. Athene was nonplussed. All she had done was give his arm a gentle squeeze. 'Heavens! Not *more* tears!' she mumbled to herself. Humdudgeon wept noisily, his shoulders shaking.

'Don't be kind to me!' he pleaded. 'I can't bear it!'

'How silly you are!' said Athene. 'Of course I'm going to be kind to you. We're friends, aren't we? Being nice to each other is what friends do!'

Humdudgeon squirmed around in the tiny, cramped space and after several attempts, managed to get his handkerchief out of his pocket and wipe his runny nose.

'You won't want to be my friend when I tell you what I've done!' he said, and a fresh bout of sobbing ensued.

'I think you'd better get it off your chest,' said Athene. 'Surely, whatever you've done can't be as bad as you're making out.'

'It is, though. It is! You see, *I lied*,' said Humdudgeon, widening his pearly eyes and staring with terror at Athene as tears continued to cascade down his face. 'Would you like to know how I really hurt my leg?' he said. 'I was chased – not by Low Gloam – but by big hairless things. They burst out of some bushes and came galumphing after me. I dashed away as fast as I could. You see, I got it in my mind that they were Gloam-eating monsters! I fell down a dozen times, tore my clothes, gashed open my leg and ended up in a ditch. Then, what do you think happened? Instead of pouncing on me and ripping me apart, my pursuers ran right past me. It was then that I saw what they really were. Not monsters at all – but hogs!'

'Hogs?' said Athene. Something stirred in her memory. She recalled Jonnie Stirrup showing her his Gloucester Old Spot pigs at Freshwater Farmhouse. Athene remembered being told that all three pigs had got out of their sty, one evening, and, like escaped convicts, they had gone on the run. The next morning, Jonnie's pigs had been found several miles away, making an awful mess of some lady's garden.

'I think I know who those hogs belonged to,' Athene said with an eager grin. 'Their names weren't Flute, Stout and Starveling, by any chance?'

'How should I know?' Humdudgeon answered irritably. 'They didn't have collars and name tags, did they?'

Athene found the whole thing quite amusing. 'You must have felt a bit silly,' she said, 'when you realised what you'd been running from. Jonnie's pigs wouldn't have done you any harm.'

'I know!' said Humdudgeon. He blew his nose. 'I felt like such a nincompoop. No self-respecting Gloam would ever run from hogs! Because of my poorly leg, it took me ages to make it back to my tribe,' he said. 'When I got there, I was muddy and bleeding, my leg could hardly bear my weight and my clothes were in rags. As soon as the others spotted me they all gathered round and asked me what had happened. I knew I'd be a laughing stock if I told them the truth, so I lied. I made up a cock and bull story about a runaway girl and three Low Gloam thugs who had given me a beating. I didn't think that anyone would find out the truth. Huffkin thought I was terribly brave and insisted on calling me a hero. It was quite nice to begin with, but after a while I started to feel like a bit of a cad.'

'The guilt got to you,' Athene said. She knew exactly what that felt like.

'If only I'd spoken up sooner,' said Humdudgeon. 'We wouldn't be down here now. My stupid made-up story made everyone think that your hare-brained plan would succeed. I'm afraid, my dear, the reality is that we're stuck down here for all time. No poor soul has ever escaped from the Low Gloam's kingdom and no one ever will.'

'I know things look quite bleak,' said Athene, 'but I'm still glad that we came.'

'Glad?' Humdudgeon said, fixing her with a horrified stare. 'How can you be glad about it?'

'If we hadn't dared to come I wouldn't have found my brother, would I?' she said, breaking into a smile. 'Zach's down here, Humdudgeon! I've seen him with my own eyes!'

'Poor little boy,' Humdudgeon said gloomily. 'He'll never see the light of day again – and why? – because I'm a worthless, cowardly louse. Huffkin detests me and when it dawns on you that I've ruined your life and your brother's as well, you'll probably hate me too.'

'No, I won't,' Athene said with certainty. Humdudgeon seemed convinced that he was the vilest creature who had ever lived and yet his wrongdoing paled into insignificance when she compared it with her own dark deed. She might have admitted that she had sent her brother into the Low Gloam's tree right there and then, but she couldn't work up the nerve.

'Come on out of there, Humdudgeon,' she said, seizing a hand and ankle and tugging him out of his badger-sized burrow. He tried to fight her off, but she was very determined.

'We need you!' she told him.

'What for?' moaned Humdudgeon, lying prostrate on the floor and rolling about as if he were in agony. 'I'm not fit for anything. I deserve to die!'

'Oh, do shut up,' said Athene, 'and listen to what I've got to say. I'm brainy, all right? I got great marks in my exams this year and I was captain of Year Seven's quiz team – but that doesn't mean I'm smart enough to think up an escape plan on my own. You're quite bright and Huffkin isn't a dimwit either. The only way that we're going to get back above ground is if all three of us put our heads *together*.'

Humdudgeon lay still. Then he sat up and clambered to his feet until he was standing beside her.

'Well?' said Athene.

'You're awfully bossy,' he said.

Six-and-a-half hours later, Athene woke up and threw off her blanket. She got dressed quickly and quietly, not wishing to awaken Huffkin and Humdudgeon who had a whole night's work ahead of them and needed to snatch every second of sleep that they could. As Athene left their quarters and hurried down the tunnel, she met no one. In the holes to either side of her, she caught brief glimpses of Gloam asleep under grey striped blankets and all manner of animals curled up in a confusion of scales, spines or fur, their ribcages rising and falling by turns.

Athene slipped out of the entrance to the Squattings seconds after the third Honk had sounded and, a little further up the tunnel, she passed the Low Gloam sentries who were wearily plodding home to their beds, having been on duty all day. They watched Athene scurry past them without interest, not bothering to call out to her or enquire where she was going. The Curfew had ended, which meant that any creature could go where they pleased as far as the sentries were concerned. If a Gloam wished to leave for work a half-hour earlier than usual it was no business of theirs.

When Athene got to the Stints, she searched several chambers until she found a handcart big enough to transport Zach. Emptying the cart of its contents (a sack of soil and a shovel), she grasped its wooden handles and steered it along the tunnel, drawing to a halt when she reached the chamber where Tippitilda worked. The Low Gloam woman was ready and waiting. She ushered Zach from the cupboard and, while Athene kept watch, lifted him into the handcart and told him to lie down.

'No wriggling about,' Tippitilda told him as she covered Zach with a blanket. 'It's really important that you stay still.'

'But I want to look at everything!' protested Zach, peeping out from underneath the blanket. His eyes shone with recently administered Goggle Drops.

'No peeking either,' said Tippitilda sternly, tucking the blanket round him. 'What happens if you're seen? Do you want to get your sister into trouble?'

'No,' breathed Zach and hid his face from view.

Tippitilda set off first and Athene waited patiently until the Low Gloam woman was far enough ahead. They had already decided that they would have to leave a certain distance between them so that they would not look as if they were accompanying each other. It was much more difficult to manoeuvre the handcart with a six-year-old boy inside. Before they had even left the Stints, Athene had almost tipped it over twice. To his credit, Zach did not make the slightest sound on either occasion.

Trying to appear as nonchalant as possible, Athene followed Tippititilda through the maze of tunnels. She could feel blisters forming on her hands as she turned the handcart this way and that. Her eyes were trained on Tippitilda's heels, which meant that she did not take much notice of the route that they were following. To her relief, they did not meet many people on their journey. One Low Gloam expressed an interest in Athene's load to which she replied, 'They're blankets, sir,' and moved swiftly on, but that encounter proved to be her closest shave. When she turned into the Digs and parked the handcart outside a round door that Tippitilda had just gone through, Athene allowed herself a smile and a huge sigh of relief.

She tugged at the bell pull and rubbed her aching arms while she waited for her fellow conspirator to answer the door.

'Yes?' said Tippitilda, emerging from her doorway. She glanced at the handcart, feigning curiosity. 'Do you have something for me, dear?'

'Your bedding has been washed and mended,' said Athene with a wink. Despite the tunnel being empty, they kept up their pretence. There was every chance that somebody might suddenly appear.

Carrying him like a rolled-up carpet, they took Zach over the threshold and into Tippitilda's living room. Only when the front door had been closed behind them did they allow him to take off the blanket.

'Cor!' Zach said, kneeling by a table and handling some figures carved in wood. 'You've got a chess set, Tippitilda!'

Athene looked around the room. 'This is very posh,' she said, trying hard not to sound envious. Apart from the low table, there was also a sofa with three plush cushions and an armchair and footstool to match. Athene yearned to sit down for a minute, but she knew that she must not. She was expected at the Sanctum in a few minutes and unless she left immediately she would be late.

'Bye! Be good,' she said to Zach, who had found a chessboard and was opening it up. 'I'll see you soon.' She loathed the idea of leaving him, but was consoled by the knowledge that he would be well provided for in Tippitilda's home. He would not have to sleep on the hard ground or have to make do with the measly portions of food dished out to the Squattings folk. He would also have more absorbing things to do than play noughts and crosses or I-Spy.

'I don't have time to take the handcart back before I go to work,' said Athene as she and Tippitilda made their way to the door. 'I'll have to ditch it somewhere and return it later. Thanks for all you've done,' she said, pausing to shake Tippitilda's hand. 'Our plan was a good one.'

'It was, wasn't it?' Tippitilda said.

And now I have to think up another one, thought Athene anxiously as she hastened to the Sanctum. It had been risky, but relatively simple to transport her brother to the Digs. Escaping from the realm of the Low Gloam was a far greater challenge and she could only hope that between them, she and her two Humble Gloam friends would be able to think of a way of achieving it. At the present moment, though she hated to admit it, she had no ideas at all.

Chapter Thirteen

Searching for the Spell

It took them three days to think of something that seemed like a workable plan. In the meantime, they all went about their jobs like good, obedient citizens.

Humdudgeon started each working day by heading straight to the Water Hole. There, he lowered buckets through the hole in the floor on a strong length of rope. When each bucket sank into the river that ran several metres beneath the chamber he would stand firm and wait until the bucket felt heavy enough; then haul it up through the hole and load it on to the cart. Finally, when all four buckets were full he would harness up Rusty and MacTavish and deliver the water to everyone who needed it. Time and again, he hauled and lifted and walked with the cart and tipped and poured and returned to the chamber to start the whole process afresh. It was a wearisome job, but it meant that he got to know every twist and turn of the tunnels and he spoke to most of the underground folk and worked out which among them were honourable and which were not to be trusted.

Huffkin's task required a lot of bending and stretching. She was given her own section of mosaic to work on, and handed a bag of stony fragments. Huffkin did not get to talk to as many people and animals as Humdudgeon did, but she learned plenty of useful information from the others in her work party. One squirrel, in particular, whose name was Skitter, was an incessant chatterer.

Athene's knowledge expanded as well. The further she delved into the Low Gloam's history, the more interested she became. She found a long chapter which went into great detail about the Battle of Barnyard Bedlam. It explained that once the Lofty Gloam (as they had previously been known) had moved from the oak tree's branches to the hayloft in a nearby barn, they had lived without incident until one moonlit autumn night. The Lofty Gloam had been going about their business in the usual way, when a pair of Glare had attacked them. It had been an unprovoked assault. The Glare had let forth with bloodthirsty cries and pelted the Gloam with missiles, which found their targets easily and caused the most dreadful injuries. As a result of their battering, the Lofty Gloam who had survived the onslaught vowed that they would relocate underground and never make themselves vulnerable to such violence again. Once they had found the hollow tree which they all agreed would make a perfect base, the burliest Gloam set about digging a shaft and a network of tunnels below it, while the others collected together all the supplies and materials that they would need for their new subterranean life. Even before the tunnels were finished they moved in, and that was when they decided to change their name from the Lofty Gloam to the Low.

'A pair of Glare?' said Athene to herself, after she had read the full account. When Tippitilda had described the battle she had made her tribe's opponents sound as numerous as a regiment. However, Athene was more convinced by the version in the book, mainly because it occurred to her that a barnyard would simply not be big enough for a major skirmish to take place there. She wondered where the battle might have been fought. It made sense for it to have happened on a local farm not unlike the one belonging to the Stirrups, which was old and had a barn and an adjacent yard. In fact, why couldn't the scene of the battle have been Freshwater Farm? Its barn was large enough to house a tribe of Gloam in its loft and there was also a sizeable tree stump in a nearby field that could conceivably be the remains of a massive, old oak – just like the tree in which the Lofty Gloam had lived before it had been felled.

Athene felt the need to prove her theory. She scrutinised the mosaic which depicted the battle on her way home from work. The mosaic did indeed feature two

Glare. They were strangely dressed, for warriors, in long flowing robes and the weapons that they wielded were unusual shapes. There were two mosaics in which the barn could be identified and the closer Athene looked at the pictures of the barn the more she was convinced that it was the very same building that stood on the Stirrups' land.

Tippitilda tired of Athene bringing up the subject of the Battle of Barnyard Bedlam whenever she stopped by at the Low Gloam's house. Zach grew weary of her obsession too. All he wanted to know was whether the plan which would take him home had been hatched yet.

'Are we getting out of here soon?' he whispered on a regular basis, whenever Tippitilda's back was turned.

It pained Athene to see him disappointed when she shook her head and told him that they were still working on it.

Kept apart during working hours, Athene and her two Gloam friends were obliged to hold their powwows after supper when most folk were settling down to sleep. After they had eaten their fill of whatever had been on the menu that day, they sat in a little circle and, in hushed voices, tried to come up with ideas that could be moulded into an escape plan. Initially, these meetings had been rather tense as Huffkin was still furious with Humdudgeon for fabricating a story to explain how he had hurt his leg. It took a lot of persuading on Athene's part to even get Huffkin to sit next to him (which, when you are sitting in a circle with two others, is not really something that you can avoid).

Huffkin ignored Humdudgeon to start off with, and then she decided to criticise every single suggestion he made. She sniped and snorted and said nasty, waspish things until the hurt and anger that had built up inside her had been well and truly vented. At their third session, Huffkin had almost reverted back to her good-natured self and Humdudgeon had begun to lose his mournful, hangdog look, which was just as well because, by this time, Athene had had quite enough of the pair of them.

The improvement in relations between the two Gloam made for a much nicer atmosphere and this, together with the fresh opinions and notions of some-body else, meant that an intelligent plan was finally hit upon.

Coney the rabbit was the ideal sort of character to be brought on board. Like all the animals Below, he had wandered into the hollow tree unsuspectingly and been grief-stricken to find himself trapped underground. He was not alone in wanting to be free again, but what set him apart from the rest of his peers was his upbeat personality and boundless energy. Coney was also very likeable and his kindness to Huffkin when she had been in need of comfort had impressed them all. Letting

Coney in on their secret soon proved to be an excellent move.

Between them, Huffkin, Humdudgeon and Athene had already worked out that they would need to break the Low Gloam's Confining Spell in order to escape, and from what Athene had told the others about her encounter with Lodestar, they guessed that the Chief's secret room was where she performed her magic. According to Humdudgeon and Huffkin, an explosion and a powerful smell were two of the things that could occur when a spell went slightly awry, and to carry out most magic (of the kind that the Low Gloam practised) you would need all sorts of ingredients and – most crucially of all – a Book of Spells.

What they needed to do was to get inside her secret room, find her Book of Spells and steal a glance at the Confining Spell which held them all prisoner. Only when Huffkin and Humdudgeon were clued up on how the spell had been performed would they be able to figure out how to reverse it.

Finding their way inside a room through a door that was hardly ever there was obviously not going to be a simple feat. Athene and her two Gloam friends had fretted about this setback, and had failed to come up with a solution. However, as soon as they had explained the problem to Coney, he saw straight away what would have to be done.

'If we can't count on the door being there, then we must make another,' he said, and he scrabbled in the dirt with his front paws, and after only a few seconds, had made quite a deep indentation in the floor.

'You're suggesting that we dig through the wall?' said Humdudgeon. 'That's a simply splendid idea! Why didn't we think of that ourselves?'

'You're a marvel, Coney, you really are,' Athene said, and she slipped her hand into her rucksack and drew out an apple. It was the last remaining piece of food from the small supply that she had brought with her. 'This is for you,' she said, placing it in front of the dumbstruck rabbit. 'Go ahead and take a nibble. You deserve it!'

They plotted for hours. It was Huffkin who finally broke up the meeting and insisted that they should all get some sleep (she had to be quite firm about it because the others were so feverish with excitement that they would have talked right through till six p.m., given half the chance).

That evening, Athene woke up earlier than usual. She put fresh Goggle Drops in her eyes and waited for Coney and his friend to turn up. It had been decided that burrowing through a wall was a tall order for just one rabbit and the likelihood of succeeding would be far greater if two sets of paws were to undertake the job.

'This is Kit,' said Coney, appearing at the mouth of the hole with another rabbit at his side.

Kit's whiskers were quivering and she could not seem to keep her ears still. She looked extremely anxious, as well she might, for it was a dangerous mission that they were about to embark on.

With a grim expression and a rapidly beating heart, Athene said her farewells to Huffkin and Humdudgeon. Then the two rabbits hopped into her rucksack, which was empty apart from her Goggle Drops and a neatly folded cardigan for Kit and Coney to sit on. She did not pull the cord tight or buckle the straps, but shifted the rucksack carefully on to her back and, taking care not to jolt its precious contents, she began the journey to Lodestar's house. When she rounded the last corner of the tunnel and spied Lodestar's guards in their familiar position either side of the entrance to the Sanctum, Athene muttered a warning to the two rabbits.

'Don't move a muscle,' she said. 'We're almost there.'

The guards were used to seeing Athene come and go, and they barely gave her a second glance as she knocked on the front door. As usual, Lodestar's servant, Dimpsy, answered it.

'So far, so good,' Athene whispered as she followed Dimpsy down the entrance hall and through several rooms until they arrived at the study. She set her rucksack gently on the floor and sat down at the desk where she always did her writing. The quill and inkpot, a fresh wad of paper and the old, tattered history book had been laid out on the desk so that she could start work straight away.

'I'll be in the scullery, if you want anything,' said Dimpsy, lingering in the doorway. 'My mistress has asked me to get on with some polishing.'

'What do you have to polish?' asked Athene. She wanted to know how long Dimpsy's chore was likely to take. Their scheme would be ruined if Dimpsy were to catch them breaking into Lodestar's secret room.

'I'm to polish the weapons that were used by the Glare during the Battle of Barnyard Bedlam,' she said.

'Oh, yes,' said Athene. 'I've read about that. It was a bit one-sided to be called a battle, I would've thought. There were only two Glare against a whole tribe of Gloam.'

'My people aren't used to combat,' said Dimpsy, 'unlike the Glare, who delight in hurting others. They're ferocious brutes. We didn't stand a chance against them.'

Athene had to bite her tongue. She hated it when the Low Gloam made the Glare out to be such monsters. Some Glare were a bit unpleasant, she could not deny that, but most of the people that she knew were courteous and friendly and not at all inclined to start a fight.

'If you hate the Glare so much, why do you keep their weapons?' asked Athene boldly. 'And why do you bother polishing them?'

'The weapons are passed down from chief to chief,'

said Dimpsy. 'They are part of our tribe's history and therefore of great value to us. They serve to remind us of the Glare's brutality and why we must always keep ourselves protected and remain below ground.'

'I suppose you've got to polish those old weapons because Lodestar is too busy to do it herself?' said Athene rather cheekily. She hoped that Dimpsy would give her a detailed answer which would tell her where Lodestar would be spending her day.

'My mistress does not do menial tasks!' said Dimpsy, frowning at the impertinence of Athene's question, 'and anyway, she's feeling out of sorts today. She's gone back to bed and doesn't want to be disturbed, so get on with your writing quietly and be sure not to make any noise.'

'I'm sorry to hear that Lodestar's feeling poorly,' said Athene. She did her best to look grave-faced and concerned, but inside she was feeling jubilant. Lodestar was tucked up in bed and in a short time, her servant would be occupied with polishing Glare artefacts in the scullery. The way was clear!

Although Athene was confident that she would not bump into anyone as she tiptoed through Lodestar's house, she kept the rabbits hidden in her rucksack until the very last minute. It would not be easy to come up with a story to explain why Kit and Coney were there, should anyone happen to see them.

Fraught with nerves, Athene got confused and did not

find the parlour as quickly as she had hoped. Once inside, she ran quickly over to the wall, where she had seen the door of the secret room magically materialise.

She lifted the flap of her rucksack and let the rabbits jump out.

'Where's the spot? Where do you want us to dig?' they clamoured, hopping round in circles and twitching their noses, eager to get started.

Athene thought very carefully before bending down and patting a place on the lowest part of the wall.

As if they were not live rabbits at all, but clockwork ones, Kit and Coney attacked the earthen wall with their front paws and scraped away soil at a remarkably fast rate. A hole appeared very quickly and after only a few minutes, all that Athene could see of the pair were the white undersides of their tails.

She crouched tensely on the floor, keeping one eye on the rabbits' tunnel and the other eye on the entrance to the room. Her main duty was to keep watch and she could not afford to get caught up in the excitement and forget that they might be discovered at any moment.

'We're through!' came Coney's muffled voice.

'Great!' said Athene softly. 'What can you see?'

'A table,' said Coney, 'and shelves with jars and pots on them. Everything is so high up!'

'A book!' said Athene urgently. 'Can you see a book?'

'No!' answered Kit. She sounded frightened. 'There

are lots of funny smells in here – and they're all *bad* smells. I don't like this place. I think we should leave.'

'Please look harder,' Athene said, fearful that Kit would panic and run back through the tunnel. 'I know it must be scary, but it's so important to find that book!'

'I think I see it!' said Coney, almost breathless with excitement.

'Can you push it through your burrow?' Athene asked. 'If I can just flick through it and find that spell . . .'

'Not a chance!' said Kit. 'It's on the table. We can only see one corner of it poking over the edge. Perhaps, if we come back tomorrow it will be in a different place. Come on, Coney, let's go.'

'No!' cried Athene, rather too loudly. 'We can't give up just yet!' She lurched forward on to her stomach intending to take a look through the tunnel that the rabbits had dug, when Kit shot out of it like a furry cannon ball.

'Coney?' called Athene, resting her head on the floor and peering into the hole. 'Is there any possible way that you can reach that book?'

She saw him crouching next to a table leg. All of a sudden the rabbit sprang upwards, his powerful hind legs propelling him into the air and out of sight. A second later, he landed. His disappointed face told Athene all that she needed to know.

'I touched it with my nose,' he said despondently, 'but all I did was push it even further on to the table top.'

Athene groaned. 'Good try,' she said. 'Oh, if only this burrow was human-sized and I could manage to crawl through!'

'I'm too tired to dig any more today,' said Kit, flopping down on the floor.

'I know,' said Athene, stroking Kit's head. 'I didn't mean to suggest that you should make the hole bigger . . . Ooh! – I've had an idea!' she said suddenly. 'There is *one* part of me that can get through that hole.'

Before either rabbit could ask her what she meant, Athene had stuck her left arm in the tunnel, all the way up to her shoulder. 'If I can just grab hold of the table leg,' she said, her fingers brushing Coney's fur. Her nails scratched around in the dirt and then, at last, she gave a cry of delight.

'Got it!'

The effort of stretching so far made her arm ache terribly but, ignoring the pain, she closed her fingers around the table's narrow leg. Concentrating with all her might, she tugged it sharply towards her. There was a scraping sound and then a thud.

Athene heard Coney make a throaty sort of growl. She withdrew her arm from the tunnel and looked through. The sight that met her eyes made her heart leap with joy. Coney was hopping across the floor with slow, clumsy movements because he was having to push a book with his nose.

Seconds later, the Book of Spells was in her hands. Athene, Coney and Kit allowed themselves a moment of self-congratulation during which the three friends shook each other's hands (or paws) with enormous glee. Then Athene opened the book's stiff, dog-eared cover and, turning the pages slowly, she searched for the spell that was keeping them trapped underground.

'The Confining Spell isn't here!' Athene said in dismay, when she had arrived at the very last page.

The rabbits expressed their astonishment.

'What?' said Coney. 'Nonsense!'

'Check again!' urged Kit.

'Well, I suppose I might have missed it,' Athene said worriedly.

The pages were old and mouldy and inclined to stick together and the writing was fanciful and hard to read. In places, the words were blurred and distorted where some sort of liquid had been spilled upon the pages. Athene leafed through the book with all the careful precision of a detective looking for clues. She was much more thorough than the first time she looked and still she could not put her finger on the spell.

'It must be here!' she said, trying her hardest to stay calm. 'I'll look again. I'm bound to find it this time.' She turned to the first page and then the second and the third. 'Spell to Cure Collywobbles . . . Spell to Give You Good Dreams . . . Spell to Loosen Tongues . . .'

'Shh!' said Coney suddenly, giving her hand a nip. 'Somebody's coming this way!'

Chapter fourteen

The Truth about the Battle of Barnyard Bedlam

If it had been Lodestar who had entered the parlour, they would have been in trouble. The Low Gloam Chief would, undoubtedly, have headed towards her secret room and noticed the small pile of earth on the floor and the rabbit burrow behind it. She might also have spotted the toes of Athene sticking out from behind the chaise longue.

However, they were in luck, because the person that entered the room was Lodestar's servant, Dimpsy, and she was so intent on carrying a tray filled with odd-shaped shiny things and not missing her footing and dropping the whole lot, that she did not seem to be aware that anything was amiss. Peering round the chaise longue, Athene saw Dimpsy set down her tray and start to transfer the objects to the shelves of a dresser. When she had finished, Dimpsy left the room, swinging the tea tray in one hand and humming to herself.

Athene breathed an enormous sigh of relief when Dimpsy had gone. Then she and the two rabbits crept out cautiously from where they had been hiding. Intending to retrieve the Book of Spells which she had hurriedly shoved beneath a small drop-leaf table, Athene crossed the room. However, before she reached the book, she could not resist pausing in front of the dresser and having a better look at the objects which she had glimpsed on Dimpsy's tray.

From their gleaming, newly polished appearance, Athene guessed that they must be the weapons that had been thrown by the Glare so many years before. Viewed from a distance, she had assumed that they were daggers and hammers and spears and other objects of that sort. It came as a bit of a shock when she saw the weapons up close. They were a bizarre collection of items, to say the least – and none of them looked as if they had been designed for use on a battlefield.

There were two saucepans (both with a number of dents in them), salt and pepper shakers, fire irons (consisting of tongs, a poker and a shovel), an egg whisk, a corkscrew and a few forks with misshapen prongs. Athene was totally mystified. She stood on tiptoe to get a better look at the items displayed on the shelves.

'How weird,' she commented, lifting out one of the

saucepans. 'These aren't weapons. They're things you'd find in a kitchen.'

'What are you doing?' demanded Coney, frustrated by Athene's inaction. 'You're wasting time! Come over here! You should be looking for the spell!' The two rabbits had already pulled the book from its hiding place. They had nudged its cover open with their noses and were in the process of turning over the pages using the same technique. Their eagerness was admirable, but the exercise was pointless as neither of them could read.

'I'll be with you in a minute,' answered Athene, examining the forks which had various marks stamped on their handles. She could not understand how the Low Gloam could believe that these kitchen implements were a haul of weapons. All the items in the dresser could be thrown, she supposed, but they weren't the sorts of missiles that you might favour if you were really dead set on causing someone harm. No one in the history books that she'd read at school had ever been dealt a fatal blow with a pepper pot or an egg whisk. It was too mind-boggling for words.

Athene started to go over in her mind all that she had learned about the Battle of Barnyard Bedlam. As she understood it, a couple of Glare had amassed a selection of kitchen utensils and had chosen to throw them at the Low Gloam tribe (or the Lofty Gloam as they had been called then) and if her hunch was right, the battle had taken place in the barnyard at Freshwater Farm.

When had Lodestar the Ninth reigned as chief of his tribe? Athene struggled to remember what had been written in the old history book. If the current chief was Lodestar the Thirteenth then that seemed to suggest that Lodestar the Ninth would have lived around a century ago or maybe even longer than that. Who would have been in residence at Freshwater Farmhouse at that time? Jonnie's grandfather, perhaps – or maybe his great-grandfather, Ishmael Stirrup, who had been the first in his family to live in the house.

Athene gasped. It wasn't just an ordinary, brief intake of breath; it was a great big, convulsive, lung-busting gulp.

Two elderly ladies called Ada and Fredegond Cheese had sold Freshwater Farm to Jonnie's ancestor, Ishmael Stirrup. Ginnie had told Athene that the old women had been frightened out of their skins by a ghostly apparition and had been so desperate to move out of their house that they had accepted an offer which was hundreds of pounds less than the house was actually worth. What if the two old ladies hadn't seen a ghost? What if they had seen a Gloam – or even more alarming than that – an entire tribe of them?

The figure two kept cropping up in the story of the Battle of Barnyard Bedlam. There were two elderly sisters, just as there were two Glare warriors and two tiny pictures of young women with old-fashioned hairstyles in the locket that hung around Tippitilda's neck. When Athene had opened the locket she had thought that the portraits looked familiar and at last she made the connection with the photograph of Fredegond and Ada in their dotage which she had seen hanging on the living room wall in Freshwater Farmhouse. The pictures of the Cheese sisters inside the locket were of young, slim, fresh-faced girls and by the time that the photograph in the farmhouse had been taken they had turned into peevish, portly old maids.

'I wonder,' muttered Athene. 'I wonder if the Cheese sisters and the Glare warriors are one and the same. I wonder if the Battle of Barnyard Bedlam was not a battle at all.'

Twirling one of the old, twisted forks in her fingers, she tried to imagine what could have happened on that night in September a hundred years before.

Having changed into their nightgowns, the Cheese sisters had delayed going to bed. Something had drawn them to the kitchen. Had they felt like a cup of cocoa, perhaps? For whatever reason, one or other of the sisters must have glanced out of the kitchen window and seen the Gloam in the barnyard. Had the sisters really believed them to be ghosts? It was arguably more likely that the Gloam had cast a spell on the old ladies which prevented them from telling the truth about what they had seen, as had been the case with Athene. Ada and Fredegond must have been gutsy old women for, despite their fear, they had seized the nearest things to hand, rushed out into the garden and flung their possessions at the Gloam to make them go away.

It had been twilight and the two old women could not have been able to see very well and, unless they had both been fast-spin bowlers in their youth, neither would they have been particularly skilful at throwing things. Athene was not convinced that the aim of Ada and Fredegond would have been quite so accurate as the Low Gloam historian had implied. How truthful was his account of the Battle of Barnyard Bedlam? He had described the Glare as hideous, sawtoothed giants whose blood-curdling war cries were enough to make a grown Gloam faint on the spot. It was evident, from their photographs, that the two sisters were a little on the plain side, but certainly not ugly or terrifying to look at. If the historian was prone to exaggeration, then perhaps there was a lot more in the Low Gloam's history book that wasn't exactly true. Had there really been dozens of Gloam who had suffered appalling injuries? How much damage could you do with a salt cellar thrown in a haphazard manner?

Confident that she had worked out what had *really* happened on the night of the Battle of Barnyard Bedlam, Athene felt enormously proud of herself, but before she could share her theories with the rabbits, she felt her

shoulder being seized and shaken roughly. Then someone whipped the fork from her grasp. Athene was
annoyed at first, but when she looked up and saw the
furious face of the person who had robbed her of the
piece of old cutlery, the only emotion that she felt was
raw, full-blown terror. Lodestar was standing in front of
her, holding the rabbits by the scruffs of their necks.
The fork protruded from her other fist.

The Chief of the Low Gloam had caught them all
red-handed.

Athene was aware that questions were being fired at her,
but she couldn't seem to make her mouth work in order
to answer them. She felt as if her brain had floated off
somewhere and left her outer shell to deal with the flack.
She could see Lodestar pacing back and forth in her
long-sleeved dress and fur-lined slippers, her necklace of
wooden beads bouncing off her bosom. Also in Athene's
line of sight, was the brawniest of Lodestar's guards. He
had been relieved of his door duty to take charge of
Coney and Kit who were wedged in the crooks of his
arms, their eyes bulging with fright. They had tried to
put up a struggle but, having just dug the burrow for
Athene, their energy reserves were low. Now that they
had exhausted themselves, they could do nothing but

hang as limply as socks on a washing line, occasionally flicking their ears. Dimpsy was there too, tying her apron strings in knots and standing near the doorway looking thunderstruck. She seemed to be unable to comprehend what was unfolding in front of her eyes.

'NEVER,' bellowed Lodestar, 'IN ALL MY YEARS AS CHIEF HAVE I HAD TO CONTEND WITH SUCH TREACHERY! What were you doing with my Book of Spells, hey? Explain yourself, you abominable girl!'

When Athene had recovered from the shock of being caught and her wits had been restored to her, she decided to stay tight-lipped. It was perfectly obvious that she and the two rabbits had broken into Lodestar's secret room and stolen her precious Book of Spells. If Athene tried to deny it she would be branded as a liar, but if she elected to admit her crime, Lodestar would be bound to ask her which spell Athene had been after and she did not want to tell her that.

In the end, the Chief resorted to magic. She slipped inside her secret room and reappeared with a beaker of viscous liquid which looked a little like cough medicine. The rabbits were ordered to swallow a spoonful each and then Lodestar chanted the Spell to Loosen Tongues (which was to be found on page three of her Book of Spells). Coney and Kit were far too weary to resist the spell and told her what she wanted to know immediately.

'So you were after *that* spell, were you?' Lodestar

crowed, glaring haughtily at Athene. She threw back her ash-white head and laughed. 'How naive you are! You won't find the Confining Spell written down in any book! It's far too important to be left lying about. The only place I keep it is inside my head,' she said, tapping her skull with her forefinger, 'and your little rabbit friends can't burrow their way in there, now can they?'

On hearing this devastating piece of news, Athene's shoulders slumped, but she would not allow herself to sulk. If she couldn't learn the secret of the Confining Spell then she would have to think of a way to win Lodestar round and persuade the Chief to break it. The Battle of Barnyard Bedlam was at the heart of her new plan. Surely, once the Low Gloam Chief was presented with the truth about the battle, she would realise that Lodestar the Ninth had made a colossal mistake in believing that all Glare were bad and thinking that it was his duty as chief to hide his people underground. If Lodestar could be persuaded that the Low Gloam would be just as safe above ground as they were below it, she would be bound to break the spell that was trapping them all in this hellish maze of musty-smelling tunnels – and everyone would be free!

Before Athene could launch into her newly formed opinions, Lodestar held up the fork in front of her astonished face. 'What is your interest in this?' said the Chief.

'I know who that used to belong to,' said Athene. 'At least, I think I do.'

'What's that?' said Lodestar. 'What did you say?' She seemed surprised, but Athene could not tell if the Chief was amazed by what Athene had just admitted or whether she was shocked because Athene had finally deigned to answer one of her questions.

'That fork that you're holding was once the property of two Glare women who were sisters,' said Athene. 'Their names were Ada and Fredegond Cheese and they were the Glare who threw all that stuff at your tribe in the little set-to that your lot insist on calling a battle. It wasn't anything nearly so momentous, in actual fact. Your historian, Ploidy, got it all wrong.'

Lodestar's face underwent a transformation. Her eyes narrowed, her nostrils flared and her lips became very thin. Athene would not have thought that a dumpy, middle-aged lady could look quite so mean and threatening.

'You DARE to criticise PLOIDY?' Lodestar thundered.

'Yes, I jolly well do,' said Athene, who was fed up with the Glare being bad-mouthed and was every bit as riled as the Chief. 'Ploidy wrote some really misleading things. He didn't bother to do much research and he made a lot of stuff up. It's Lodestar the Ninth who is most to blame, though. He got the wrong end of the stick *completely* . . .'

'ENOUGH!' roared Lodestar. 'Curb your tongue! I forbid you to utter another word!'

'You're just mad because you know I'm talking sense,' murmured Athene obstinately. She hated being told to shut up.

'You will be quiet instantly,' warned the Chief, 'or I might be tempted to use this deadly weapon to silence you.' She lunged at Athene with the fork, but stopped short of actually jabbing her with it.

'You're cuckoo, you know that?' Athene said. 'You're a complete nut. These objects that you've got on display aren't weapons. They're things that you'd find in a kitchen. Any Glare could tell you that, but you Gloam haven't got the slightest clue. It's not your fault, I suppose. You can't have come across fire irons before, not having wanted to ever light a fire and you wouldn't know what a saucepan is either because you don't eat food that's cooked. Still, when someone goes to the trouble of trying to put you straight you might show some manners and listen without interrupting.'

'DIMPSY!' roared the Chief, turning to her servant. 'Run and fetch help. Now! Right this minute! This young woman needs restraining!'

Dimpsy dithered for a moment. She did not seem to want to leave. It took another barked command from Lodestar before she nodded and ran from the room. In the meantime, Lodestar's guard seemed in two minds what to do. He could not come to Lodestar's aid without releasing his hold on the rabbits and as soon as he placed them on the floor, their paws scrabbled feverishly and they tried to scramble away.

'What do you think you're doing?' said Lodestar, frowning at the guard. 'Hold on to those traitorous rabbits. Don't let them escape!'

'But what about the girl?' said the guard, struggling to hold the squirming rabbits in his arms.

'I can handle her for the moment,' the Chief informed him, making slashing motions in the air with the fork. 'She doesn't dare move while I have this.'

'Don't be silly!' said Athene. 'If you were to prod me with that fork it might hurt a bit, but it wouldn't cause much damage. You use it to eat with. It's certainly not a weapon!'

Knowing that it was important to get her timing right, Athene waited until Lodestar waved the fork near enough for her to grab hold of it. When she shot out her arm to snatch it, Lodestar was taken unawares.

'I'll show you what you do with it,' Athene said, whipping the fork away and pretending to eat with it.

'You nasty little thief!' screamed Lodestar, snatching a handful of Athene's hair and yanking it so hard that Athene's scalp smarted with the pain.

Athene tried to retaliate, but the Chief's hair was too short to get a satisfactory grip on it. She decided to give

Lodestar a firm shove instead.

They might have grappled with each other for several minutes more if Dimpsy had not returned with Lodestar's other guard in tow. The guard overpowered Athene with the minimum of effort, pinning her arms behind her back. With one hand, he seized her wrists and with the other, he opened Athene's palm and took the fork away from her.

'Good,' said Lodestar, panting slightly. She straightened her dress and smoothed her hair which had got quite messed up in the scuffle. When she had made herself presentable she accepted the fork which the guard was holding out to her.

'Take charge of this unruly creature, will you?' she said to the guard. 'Be sure to have your wits about you. She's very unpredictable. There have been others amongst us who have not adapted to our way of life and have succumbed to hysteria. However, I don't remember anyone losing control like this young Gloam. Don't be deceived by her innocent looks,' warned Lodestar, shaking a finger, 'and don't feel any pity for her either. She's crafty, cunning and dangerous.'

The guard gave Athene a distrustful glare and gripped her wrists even more tightly.

'Now, take her away,' said Lodestar, wrinkling up her nose to show her displeasure.

'But you can't!' Athene protested. 'I won't go. Not

yet! Not until you've heard me out. The Glare that attacked your people all those years ago weren't warriors at all and they weren't bad people either. They were a pair of scared old ladies. If you ask Tippitilda to open up her locket you'll see their pictures. You don't have to be afraid of the Glare and there isn't any need to live underground! Don't you see? The whole thing's just a silly misunderstanding.'

'Twaddle,' said Lodestar dismissively, smiling at Athene as if she were a simpleton. 'Exactly the sort of ludicrous bilge I'd expect from someone who's raving mad – and that's what I've decided you are.'

'The Glare aren't horrible!' Athene shouted, frustrated by Lodestar's refusal to take her seriously. 'Why won't you listen to what I'm saying?'

'Must you persist in defending the Glare?' snapped Lodestar, losing her temper. 'They are our sworn enemies. How can you pretend to know so much about them?'

'Because I'm a Glare myself,' Athene said, struggling to stop herself from being bundled across the room.

'Are you trying to tell me that you're part Glare?' said the Chief. The laugh that escaped from her lips was hollow and disbelieving.

'No, I'm Glare through and through,' declared Athene. The situation was getting so desperate that she no longer cared about pretending to be a Gloam. 'There isn't a single drop of Gloam blood running in my veins,' she boasted, hoping that this bombshell would herald some sort of breakthrough and prove once and for all that the Low Gloam's terrible opinion of the Glare was grossly undeserved.

'Of all the ridiculous nonsense!' scoffed Lodestar, glancing at the others. 'As I suspected – this girl is clearly deranged. Don't stand there gawping, Dimpsy. All the excitement is finished with. Go and get on with your chores, please. Guards, remove this crackpot and her two associates. You know where to take them.'

'Where?' said Athene, trying to resist being dragged out of the door. 'Answer me!' she said fiercely.

'Where all troublemakers are taken,' said the Chief in a cool, dismissive voice. 'To the Coop, of course.'

Chapter fifteen

Cooped Up

Coney and Kit were much lighter and a lot more cooperative than Athene and so the guard that carried them led the way. Athene brought up the rear of their little procession, dragged along by the other Low Gloam guard. Determined to be as much of a nuisance as she could and thus delay her arrival at the Coop, Athene refused to walk for more than a couple of paces at a time before sinking to the ground as if her legs would not support her weight. This was annoying for the guard, but it was also painful for Athene (and for her knees in particular) because he refused to stop. Keeping a firm hold on her wrists, the guard dragged Athene beside him, unmoved by her cries of protest. Eventually, tiring of her stubbornness, he swept Athene up in his arms and carried her in a fireman's lift, which frustrated her efforts at slowing him down and also made it hard for her to observe the route that they were taking. Athene thumped his back with her fists and tried to waggle her legs, but the guard continued to plod along at a steady pace and took no notice.

Their journey ended at the bottom of a flight of steps. When Athene's feet had been planted on the ground again she was able to take in her new surroundings. They had arrived in a chamber with a low roof and a few basic items of furniture: a bench, a table with some dirty plates on it and a bed with a pillow and a blanket that had both been patched and mended. There appeared to be only one other prisoner there: a gaunt, gangly man, with long greasy hair and bulbous eyes that never seemed to blink. He stood and watched them keenly.

Athene was mildly relieved by what she saw. The chamber was not decked out in mod cons, of course, but it was clean and dry and did not appear to be as grotty as the guards had described. Perhaps it would not be such a bad place to be imprisoned. Cautiously, she ventured further in.

When Athene noticed that the chamber had a hard, rocky floor she was reminded of the Water Hole. To her amazement, this chamber also had a hole in its centre; only instead of being exposed, this hole had a crude sort of grating covering it. Athene approached the hole, curious to know what resided in its depths. She wondered if there might be a river running below it, like the one in the Water Hole.

'That's right, ducky,' simpered the Gloam with greasy

hair. 'Take a teeny peek, why don't you? 'Course you might see better if you lift off the lid. That's the way, sweetie-pie. Careful not to trap your precious little fingertips!'

The lid was like a circular drain cover, constructed from wood rather than metal which made it manageable for Athene to shift. She pulled the cover to one side, knelt beside the hole and looked down it. There were no glimmering ripples below and no sounds of fast-flowing water. Instead, Athene was startled to hear a chorus of pitiful cries. Staring up at her, she glimpsed a number of fearful, anxious faces.

'In you pop!' said a voice in her ear. Before she could stop him, the long-haired man had pushed Athene out of the way. To her horror, one after the other, he dropped the two rabbits into the hole.

'Don't!' she said, clasping the rim of the hole and staring wildly into it. 'Coney! Kit!' she called. 'Are you all right?'

'Just about!' answered Coney, sounding a little shaken. 'Luckily, some kind people caught us before we hit the ground.'

'Why'd you do that?' said Athene, turning to the long-haired man.

'Oops!' he said, smirking. 'Clumsy me!'

'You did that on purpose,' Athene said, shrinking away from him. 'You're not a prisoner at all, are you?

How could I be such an idiot? This room isn't the Coop, is it? That's the Coop down there,' she said, pointing towards the hole.

The man's delighted giggle made the hairs stand up on the back of her neck.

'Your turn next,' he said, holding out his knobbly fingers and creeping slowly towards her. 'Come along, poppet. You mustn't be naughty. Don't you want to join your little friends?'

'Watch out, Scabbler,' warned the nearest guard. 'She's a loony and likely to give you trouble.'

'Thank you for your advice,' said Scabbler witheringly. 'I think I can manage a slip of a girl. You're dismissed. Go on. I said you could leave!'

The two guards shrugged at each other and rolled their eyes. Then they wished Scabbler luck, told him he'd need it, and left.

Athene backed into a corner. She did not want to be put in the Coop where, if the guards had been telling her the truth, bugs crawled all over you while you slept. Sick of being labelled as a mad person and fed up with the Glare being demonised, she had had more than enough of the injustice of it all. As Scabbler sidled closer, she made up her mind that she would live up to the undeserved reputation of the Glare and fight him off as best she could.

She gave him a Chinese burn when he tried to seize

her wrist and followed that up with a punch to the stomach and a kick in the shins. Caught off guard, Scabbler's reflexes proved to be too slow and he let Athene dodge past him and wrench open the door to the chamber. Without stopping to close it, she began her ascent of the steps. Behind her, she heard Scabbler laughing and then he shouted something that tested Athene's resolve.

'Run, my pretty,' he called. 'How far do you think you will get in a place that has no exit? You'll be caught and brought back here. It's a shame that you chose to attack me. I shall have to make you suffer for that! Run by all means, sweet one, but you'll never get away!'

His words dampened her spirits, but Athene was not so disheartened that she gave up all hope of avoiding recapture. Putting as much distance between her and the Coop and its creepy jailer was the overriding aim in her mind. She regretted having to leave Coney and Kit behind, but she knew that she would be of more use to them as an escapee than a fellow prisoner.

Desperation and fear gave Athene extra energy and she reached the top of the steps in five seconds flat. Not wishing to run the risk of bumping into Lodestar's guards, she took a different route from the one which they had chosen to bring her to the Coop. Unsure of where she was heading, Athene's only goals were to evade anyone who tried to stop her and to keep on kitchen utensils, you say? I'm not surprised that Lodestar had difficulty swallowing that.' Huffkin shook her head sadly, a pained look of disbelief on her face. 'It's tragic really, isn't it?' she said. 'If Lodestar the Ninth hadn't panicked . . . if someone in the Lofty Gloam had shown a bit of common sense . . . if they'd been a little less hasty they wouldn't have hidden themselves underground needlessly for all these years.'

When Athene broke the news that the two rabbits had been imprisoned and that she had only just managed to avoid the same fate, Huffkin's expression grew even more sorrowful.

'Dear, dear,' said the Gloam, her hands clasping her cheeks. 'We're in a pretty pickle now. I can't see a way out of it.'

With little time to waste, they decided to find Humdudgeon. There wasn't much chance that he'd be able to come up with an answer to their problems, but they both thought that they would feel a bit braver in his company. They did not dare to visit Tippitilda for fear that it would lead Lodestar straight to Zach. Athene could not bear to think of her brother being thrown in the Coop, not after everything he had suffered already.

They found Humdudgeon in the Water Hole. He did not notice them at first. He was engaged in a hushed conversation with Rusty and MacTavish. The tails of the dog and the fox were sweeping from side to side and running until she found a friend.

In her panicked state, she would have run right past Huffkin, if the Gloam had not jumped into her path and called her name.

'Thank goodness I've found you,' said Huffkin, giving Athene a hug and pulling her along the tunnel until they found a secluded section where they could talk without being overheard.

'Things haven't gone according to plan,' Athene said.

'I guessed as much,' said Huffkin. 'I heard a rumour that a Gloam had upset Lodestar and had been seen being hauled down a tunnel by a guard.'

'That was me,' said Athene, showing Huffkin the grazes on her knees.

Huffkin made sympathetic noises. 'I've been hunting for you everywhere. Not long ago, I came across your bag lying on the floor . . .'

'I must've dropped it without realising,' said Athene, taking her rucksack from Huffkin and hooking her arms through the straps. 'It must have happened when that beast of a guard was pulling me along. Thanks a lot. I would've been lost without my Goggle Drops.'

'So, what went wrong?' asked Huffkin.

As briefly as she could, Athene filled her in. She also explained how she had come to the conclusion that the Battle of Barnyard Bedlam had not been a battle at all.

'Two old ladies?' said Huffkin in total shock, 'and

when they caught sight of Huffkin and Athene their tails wagged even more.

Humdudgeon had taken his workmates into his confidence and told them about the plan to escape. Even when Rusty and MacTavish learned that the plan had gone wrong, MacTavish continued to trot about excitedly. He behaved like a different dog from the miserable soul that Athene had first encountered. He kept nudging them all with his nose and telling them about his owners, who were a young couple called the Winstanleys. Rusty was not quite as thrilled as her canine friend until Athene thought to mention that fox-hunting had now been banned. It did not seem to matter to Rusty or MacTavish that the chances of getting above ground were slim. The mere mention of an escape plan had an amazing effect on their moods.

They had not even begun to discuss what they should do next when Huffkin gave them a warning. She had been posted as lookout at the mouth of the chamber and by her frantic hand signals, which insisted that they should button their lips, it was quite clear that someone was coming.

'Low Gloam,' hissed Huffkin. 'And they don't look friendly.'

Athene was panic-stricken. She looked around for somewhere to conceal herself, but the chamber had no nooks or crannies to crawl into. If she crouched behind the buckets in the cart, she'd be discovered in less than half a minute. Her stomach lurched when she realised that the cart was her only option.

There was nowhere else to hide.

Chapter Sixteen

A Bucketful of Terror

Quicker than Athene had ever seen him move, Humdudgeon darted over to where a length of rope was coiled untidily on the floor. He seized one end of the rope and knotted it firmly around his waist. Then he searched frantically for the other end and knotted that to the handle of a bucket.

'Right,' said Humdudgeon, giving Athene a brisk nod. 'In you get, my dear. Look sharp.'

'I don't think I'm small enough to fit in there,' said Athene, wondering how Humdudgeon could expect her to squeeze herself inside a container that barely reached above her knees.

'Don't be scared,' Humdudgeon said. 'You'll be quite safe.' He bunched the rest of the rope in his hands and altered his stance so that his feet were planted firmly and his knees were slightly bent.

Athene looked at the rope and then at the sturdy wooden bucket to which it had been attached. Finally her eyes slid to the hole in the rocky floor. A second later, the penny dropped and she caught on to what he was suggesting. 'You want me to dangle above the river in that bucket? That's a bonkers idea,' she said.

At that moment, MacTavish started to bark. He had rushed to join Huffkin at the entrance of the chamber when she had announced that a group of Low Gloam were drawing near. His hackles were up, his ears were erect and his tail was as straight as a radio aerial. Every time he gave a resounding woof, his front paws left the floor.

Huffkin looked over her shoulder and pulled a face at Humdudgeon. 'They're nearly here,' she said in a loud whisper. 'Why are you messing around with that bucket? You should be helping Athene to hide!'

'That's exactly what I *am* doing!' Humdudgeon said.

Athene hesitated. She heard the footsteps of the Low Gloam pounding down the tunnel.

'Oh, all right,' she said to Humdudgeon. 'You'd better not drop me, though.'

Rusty looked on with a concerned expression as Humdudgeon lowered the bucket into the hole and, standing well back from the edge, told Athene to step inside it. She did so slowly and carefully, gripping the rope with both hands. Humdudgeon puffed out his cheeks with the effort of holding her weight, then let the rope feed through his fingers so that she started to descend.

Athene heard the sound of a kerfuffle at the entrance to the chamber. She guessed that Huffkin and MacTavish were attempting to waylay the Low Gloam, but she did not see what happened next. The hole swallowed her up and before she knew it, she had passed through the narrow opening and was dangling precariously near the roof of a cave with a body of water flowing beneath her.

She did not know what was going on in the chamber above. The river was making too much noise as it rushed on its journey for her to hear the voices of her friends or foes. All she could see was a small cave with craggy, glistening walls and a river like a moving, gleaming carpet taking up all the space on its floor.

Athene was sure that the group of Low Gloam, whom she had narrowly managed to avoid, had been despatched to look for her. She hoped that they would carry out a quick search of the chamber and be satisfied that she was not there. With any luck, they would take one look at Humdudgeon and assume that he was in the middle of hauling up a bucket of water. Athene hoped that his strength held out. She reckoned that it must be an awful strain to suspend a person in mid-air.

Keeping her balance was essential. She maintained a tight hold on the rope and did not move a single toe, hoping that her stillness would make things easier for Humdudgeon. Athene did not want to fall out of the bucket. Although it was only a short drop and swimming was a sport that she was fairly good at, she did not relish the thought of taking a dip in a cold, fast-flowing river with no lifebelts to hand and little chance of getting out again.

Looking at the river made her nervous, but there was nothing else for her to do. Its fluid surface rippled like a length of wind-blown silk and its speed was surprisingly swift. Athene found herself wondering what might happen if she let the river carry her on its underground journey. At some point, the river had to emerge into the open. What would happen then? Would Lodestar's spell stretch quite that far and if it did, might the flow of the river be strong enough to propel a person along and break through the spell's boundary? As the minutes ticked by, the idea of swimming to freedom became more and more attractive and by the time that Huffkin's voice delivered the welcome news to Athene that the Low Gloam had gone, she had convinced herself that her daring plan had every chance of succeeding.

'Humdudgeon's going to pull you up!' yelled Huffkin. 'Hold on tight!'

'No! Wait!' Athene replied. Her voice echoed around the cave. 'There's something I need to do. Ask Humdudgeon to let out the rope. I have to go lower.'

There was silence. Then Athene heard Huffkin's voice again. 'Humdudgeon wants to know what you're playing at,' she said. 'He says that his arms are going to fall off if he has to hold on to you for much longer.'

'Please!' called Athene. 'I wouldn't ask if it wasn't important.'

A few seconds later, Athene felt the bucket drop jerkily little by little. She held on to the rope for dear life.

'Lower!' shouted Athene.

The bucket descended a fraction more, stopping just above the ruffled surface of the river.

'That's low enough!' yelled Athene. She looked to her left, to where the river entered the cave through a jagged archway. Her eyes followed its course, along the cave floor and through another archway to her right. At this level she was able to get a much better view. Her plan to swim to freedom relied upon there being adequate head-room between the river's surface and the rocky roof. If the roof touched the water at any point, then the swimmer would be forced to continue underwater and if the level of the roof did not rise again for a considerable distance there was a chance that the swimmer might drown.

There were no glowing stones in the cave and Athene found that she couldn't see as clearly as normal. She peered into the right-hand archway, trying to ascertain if there was plenty of space between the river's surface and the roof. In her attempt to get a good look, she let go of the rope with one hand and leaned out over the river.

The bucket trembled and the rope started to twist.

Suddenly Athene felt the bucket drop and heard a loud smack as it collided with the water. It seemed as though Humdudgeon's strength had given out. She struggled to keep her balance, but was not able to. The bucket began to slide as if it had been placed on a conveyor belt and, despite her best efforts to stay upright, Athene toppled out. Her scream was amplified in the tiny cave. With a tremendous splash, she hit the water.

Its icy temperature took her breath away. When her head plunged under the surface, she had the good sense to squeeze her eyes tightly shut. Her Goggle Drops had been washed out of her eyes once before in a rainstorm and she did not want that to happen again, especially not while she was at the mercy of an underground river.

The water that filled her ears and blocked her nose ran out again when her face broke through the surface of the water. Instinctively, her arms flailed around and her feet kicked out. She tried to find something solid on which to anchor herself, but the river was too deep for her to find its bottom. As if she were no heavier than a piece of driftwood, the river carried her along. She drew closer and closer to the right-hand archway until she had almost reached it and it was then that she saw quite clearly that only a little further downstream the rocky roof dipped down to meet the river. The realisation that her plan was not likely to work made her squawk with fear. The water frothed as her arms and legs went into overdrive, but her frenzied attempts to swim upstream were in vain. The river's current was far too powerful.

'I don't want to drown!' cried Athene. 'Help! Somebody help me!'

The archway loomed ahead of her until she found herself floating underneath it, towards the low roof and the awful possibility that she would never resurface again. Athene was terror-struck. At the last moment, she summoned the strength to reach up and grab a spike of jutting rock. She felt the river push against her, jostling her like a heaving crowd, trying to drag her with it, but Athene hung on with all her might, determined not to be dislodged. Then, with a great snort of effort, she grasped the rock with her other hand. In the next minute she found a foothold on the side of the archway and wedged her toes into it. Water streamed from her hair and her clothes as she pulled herself out of the river and found a crevice in which to put her other foot. She rested for a few seconds, worn out by her exertions. Then, with slow, cautious movements, feeling her way across the rugged wall of the cave, Athene edged closer to the bucket, which was still attached to the rope. She managed to draw level with the bucket, which was being buffeted by the water, but the problem still remained of how to get to it. There was no chance of reaching the bucket if she leaped from the wall. The distance was too far. Her muscles hurt, her knees were sore and her fingers were bleeding. She was cold and wet and beginning to despair when she heard a voice and, looking round, saw Huffkin shinning down the rope with the agility of a gymnast. They stared at each other desperately.

'I can't make it,' said Athene, gulping back tears. She had never felt so frightened in her life.

'Yes, you can!' insisted Huffkin.

'My fingers are slipping!' Athene wailed.

'Hold on!' said Huffkin. 'Listen, Athene . . . here's what you'll have to do: move three metres to your left.'

'What good will that do?' said Athene, unwilling to ask her tired limbs to do any more clambering.

'You must get back into the water,' said Huffkin. 'Go a bit further along the wall and then you'll have to jump. Try and swim into the middle of the river, as close to the bucket as you can get, and then when you pass by, I'll grab hold of you.'

It was a risky plan. If anything went wrong, Athene doubted that she would have the energy to stop herself from being pulled through the archway.

'I don't suppose you know a spell that could help me to breathe underwater,' she said.

'Even Lodestar wouldn't know a spell like that!' replied Huffkin.

'You're right,' said Athene with a sigh. She didn't recall seeing such a spell in Lodestar's Book of Spells and she had been all the way through it twice. Athene made an attempt at a smile. 'That leaves me with no choice, then. Will Humdudgeon be able to manage the weight of both of us?'

'Don't you worry your head about that,' said Huffkin as she slid down the last portion of rope and dropped into the bucket, which wobbled until she found her balance.

Gingerly, Athene manoeuvred herself along the wall, clinging to every notch and groove with her fingertips and grazing her legs against the coarse rock as she struggled to find new footholds. On more than one occasion, she had to work her way around stalactites, which hung down like giant icicles from the roof and made her job even more difficult. After a quarter of an hour had passed, Athene stopped. She had not managed to get quite as far as Huffkin had wanted her to, but she did not feel as if she could cleave to the wall for a moment more.

'I'm ready to jump,' she told Huffkin and, trying not to think of the consequences should she sail past the bucket and slip through Huffkin's grasp, Athene let herself fall. Once again, she got a shock as the freezing cold water closed over her head. Then she bobbed to the surface and began to swim front crawl, which was her strongest stroke. When she thought that she had reached the middle of the river, she trod water, her eyes fixed on the bucket and Huffkin's outstretched arms. The Gloam had bravely let go of the rope and was kneeling in the bucket, which was tipping at an alarming angle. Huffkin leaned towards Athene and shouted words of encouragement, as the gap between them grew narrower and narrower.

'You can do it! Hold your hand up,' she said. 'Stretch a bit higher. That's it!'

Their fingers touched and then gripped hard. For a few critical seconds, they clung to each other and fought against the current which was trying its best to part them. Then Huffkin pulled Athene's hand towards her and pressed it to the rim of the bucket. Athene's other hand joined it, but she only had enough strength to hold on. She was so exhausted that she could not lift herself out of the water and, try as she might, Huffkin could not manage to heave Athene and her waterlogged clothes into the bucket without help.

'Pull us up!' cried Huffkin, turning her face to the hole in the roof. Her hands fastened around her friend's forearms and she advised Athene to hang on like grim death and not let go.

It seemed to take an age for them to be hauled to safety. Athene closed her eyes and gritted her teeth and clung on tightly, even though her arms felt as if they were being torn from their sockets. She made all sorts of distressed noises, but at long last she heard the bottom of the bucket hit the floor of the chamber and felt eager hands seize her arms and sharp teeth tug at her clothes and when she had been extricated from the hole, she rolled on to her back and cried tears of relief.

It was only when her eyes had received more Goggle Drops that she realised exactly who her rescuers were. Humdudgeon was standing in the same position with the rope knotted around his waist, but standing at his side were Shoveller the badger, Rusty, MacTavish and a fox she did not know, all of whom were spitting strands of rope from their mouths and licking their bleeding gums. Kneeling by the hole with smiles on their faces were two people that Athene had definitely not expected to see.

'How are you feeling?' said Tippitilda, her face flushed and her dress darkened by river water which had dripped from Athene's clothes when her friends had dragged her from the hole.

Zach simply launched himself at his sister and gave her a hug. He smelt rather odd and when Athene let go of his shoulders and looked at him she saw that an attempt had been made to give him Gloam-like markings on his face.

'Is that Blend?' Athene asked, rubbing her finger across his cheek.

'No – ink,' said Tippitilda. 'When Rusty told me that you were in a fix, I thought I'd better drop in and tell Zach. Of course, he wanted to come and help. His disguise is rather patchy, I'm afraid. He was so eager to get to you . . . he was out of the door before I'd finished.'

'I'm going to need more Goggle Drops,' said Athene, laughing, as she felt her eyes filling with tears again.

When it came to digging holes, Shoveller was an expert. The hole that he dug for Athene in the wall of the chamber where her friends had assembled to rescue her, was just the right size for a girl of her height. Once she had wriggled through its entrance tunnel, she found that she could sit upright without bumping her head on its ceiling and getting dirt in her hair and when she felt like a nap she discovered that there was plenty of room to lie down and even roll over if she wanted to.

Shoveller had hardly rested for a moment after helping to pull on the rope and haul up the bucket which Athene had been hanging from. Realising how urgent it was for a hiding place to be found for her, he had chosen a spot in the nearest wall and set to work straight away. It was only when he had scooped out the final pawful of earth that he sank on to his haunches and took a well-deserved breather. By that time, the chamber had emptied somewhat. The lean, rangy fox with a torn ear and a white-tipped tail whose name, Athene learned, was Fleet, had gone back to his job of licking dirty plates clean and Tippitilda had thought it wise to return Zach to her house in the Digs. Before they had gone, Athene had let them know how indebted she felt towards them. When Rusty had shown up in a frightful panic with the news that Athene was in mortal danger, each of them had stopped what they were doing and rushed to her aid. Their prompt actions had undoubtedly saved her life. Without their assistance, it was questionable whether Rusty, MacTavish and a totally frazzled Humdudgeon would have had the muscle power to pull her out of the water.

When Athene settled down to sleep, she had the security of knowing that the entrance tunnel to her hole had been filled in with earth, making it indistinguishable from the rest of the chamber wall. Should the Low Gloam search the Water Hole again, they would be unlikely to notice it. As she laid her head on her folded-up cardigan she felt at peace. Zach was still safe, she had got away from Scabbler and evaded capture for several hours and although she felt a pang of sadness when she thought about Coney and Kit in the Coop, she felt hopeful that a new day would bring better things.

Athene awoke several hours later and sneezed. The air smelled damp and when she touched the soil around her, it felt moist as well. When she mentioned this to Rusty later on, the fox seemed to think that there must have been a shower of rain up above and sure enough, when Humdudgeon lowered the first of his buckets into the river, he commented that the water level seemed to have risen considerably.

'You don't think that the river could rise so high it'd come through the hole in the floor?' said Athene, shuddering at the thought.

Humdudgeon smiled and shook his head. 'It would take a veritable torrent to do that,' he said.

'This *is* England,' Athene reminded him. 'It could happen.'

'Perhaps you should pray that it does,' said Humdudgeon. Water slopped from a bucket as he lifted it into the cart. 'If we had a flood down here it might shock that stubborn old Low Gloam Chief into breaking the Confining Spell.'

Athene's eyes opened wide. 'Humdudgeon, you're an absolute genius,' she said.

Chapter Seventeen

A Dam and a Blast

They scheduled the next meeting of the escape committee for after suppertime. An overexcited Athene as keen to call the group together right there and then, ut Humdudgeon persuaded her to wait. He pointed out at it was quite usual for everyone to take strolls after pper, but if a Gloam or animal suddenly took off when ey were meant to be working, it might make the Low loam wonder what they were up to. Between suppertime and the beginning of the Curfew had seemed a od time for a powwow. They could not be any more ecific than that because they had only got one wristatch between them and that belonged to Athene and its nds had not budged at all since her prolonged dip in e River Axe. It was wearying for Athene to have to treat inside her den and endure several more hours of litude while she waited for her friends to finish their bs and turn up at the Water Hole. After what seemed e a week she heard Humdudgeon call her name and in

227

seconds he had scraped away the earth which conceale
the entrance to Athene's new home. She wriggled ou
immediately and they greeted each other warmly.

'I've brought my set of tools,' Humdudgeon said, 'an
I managed to perform that Multiplying Spell that yo
were telling me about.' He unbuttoned his jacket an
revealed an impressively long length of rope, which h
had wound around his body so that no one would se
him carrying it. 'Huffkin's bringing more,' he said, 'an
there's another lot stashed somewhere safe.'

'You did a spell without permission?' Athene sai
'That was risky. No one saw you do it, did they?'

'Well, of course not,' Humdudgeon answered with
sneer. 'As if I'd be that stupid!'

Huffkin arrived in the chamber a short while aft
Humdudgeon. She looked rather dusty and tired an
cross. 'Our hole keeps being ransacked,' she told Athen
'I've lost count of the times I've tidied things up. Tho
beastly Low Gloam! Oh, bother. I've clean forgotten t
rope Humdudgeon asked me to bring.'

'Those Low Gloam won't give up the search for you
said Rusty the fox, padding gracefully over to Athe
and taking a seat beside her. The fox placed her fro
paws together and curled her tail around them tidi
rather like a domestic cat. 'Lodestar is in the most fearf
temper. She's issued an order that everyone should lo
for you. The Low Gloam are doing their bit, of cours

but the rest of us are only pretending to look. They think it's a marvellous joke that someone's managed to outwit the Low Gloam Chief!'

'There's a rumour going round that you're a powerful magician and you've made yourself invisible,' MacTavish said, glancing in Athene's direction for the briefest of moments. He had volunteered to stand guard at the entrance to the chamber and he was taking his duty very seriously. His short black ears were permanently pricked and every few seconds he sniffed the air to check that no unwelcome visitors were approaching.

'Good evening, friends,' he said, when Shoveller and Fleet arrived together.

'Sorry we're late,' said Fleet. 'We came upon a wall full of succulent earthworms. Excuse our bad manners. We shouldn't have gobbled them all ourselves. Next time we'll be sure to share them with you.'

Athene smiled but said nothing.

'Are we all here?' asked Huffkin, turning a bucket upside down and perching on it.

'What about Zach and Tippitilda?' Athene said.

'I didn't think that it was safe to ask Tippitilda,' admitted Humdudgeon. 'She's a Low Gloam, don't forget.'

Athene was indignant. 'But Tippitilda helped save me from drowning and she promised to keep my hiding place a secret!'

'That's because she likes you,' said Humdudgeon, patting Athene's knee. 'She's prepared to be a bit disloyal to her tribe if it means that you'll be safe, but I hardly think she'd be willing to give her blessing to our escape plan. She'd blow the whistle on us, I'm certain of it.'

Athene grumbled about this decision, because she had come to trust Tippitilda. However, she was forced to concede that it would be foolish to take any risks at such an early stage.

'So, what *is* this plan of yours?' asked Shoveller. He lumbered over to the little group who were seated in a circle behind the cart, plonked himself down and began to inspect his hairy belly for fleas.

'It's a top idea,' Athene said. 'Humdudgeon thought of it.'

'I may have had the first inklings, but you were the one that seized upon them, my dear,' said Humdudgeon and they grinned at each other. Having praised each other's ingenuity, they finally got round to explaining the essence of their plan.

'We're going to flood the tunnels!' said Athene, revelling in the astonishment on everybody's faces.

'And how do you intend to do that?' asked Fleet.

'We're going to build a dam,' said Humdudgeon. 'We thought we'd block the path of the river so that it gushes up through that hole over there. The Low Gloam's kingdom will disappear under water.'

Shoveller rolled over into a standing position. 'Never mind how you're going to do it,' he bellowed, squaring up to Humdudgeon and giving him a threatening poke with one of his claws, 'why would you ruddy well want to? Are you totally crackbrained, the pair of you? We'll all be drowned!'

'It doesn't sound like the *best* idea you've ever had,' said Huffkin, gazing confusedly at her fellow Gloam. 'I don't really see how *escaping* comes into it.'

'Ah, that's the clever part!' Humdudgeon said, backing away from the badger who looked as if he might fly at him at any moment. 'Lodestar will *think* that we'll all be drowned so she'll break the secret spell to save our lives.'

'Once the spell's been broken we'll be able to go Above,' said Athene.

Shoveller grunted. 'How?' he said.

'We can climb up the shaft,' Athene told him. 'We've got loads of rope.'

Obligingly, Humdudgeon revealed the sturdy length of cord that he had concealed under his jacket.

'And what about us?' said Rusty glumly. 'Paws aren't any use for climbing!'

'We were hoping that you'd dig us some tunnels,' said Athene, resting her hand on the fox's neck. 'You, MacTavish, Fleet and Shoveller. We'll need plenty of escape routes to give everyone a good chance of getting out.'

'Hmph,' said Shoveller, sitting back down. 'It could work, I suppose.' He gave Humdudgeon a reluctant nod. 'All right, I'll go along with it. Count me in,' he said.

'Let's have a show of hands,' said Humdudgeon. There was disgruntled murmuring. 'Or paws,' he said and muttered a hasty apology. 'Who votes that we should give our plan a try?'

Apart from MacTavish who raised his paw immediately and Shoveller who had already made up his mind, the others took several minutes to decide. Their desperate longing to escape was countered by their fear that Lodestar, stubborn harridan that she was, would not agree to break the spell. It was only when Shoveller delivered a rousing speech, urging them to show what they were made of and give their support to the only escape plan that anyone had had the imagination to think up that the tide of opinion began to turn.

'But if Lodestar digs her heels in, and everybody drowns – it will be our fault,' wailed Huffkin, dropping the hand that she had begun to raise.

'I'd rather die trying,' declared Shoveller, 'than be stuck in this cheerless place for the rest of my life, dreaming of the great open spaces and the sweet-smelling grass and all my dear old mates and knowing that I could have got back above ground if only I'd been brave enough.'

This last announcement of Shoveller's seemed to win

them over. One by one, they indicated that, despite the obvious dangers, they would back the plan.

'It's unanimous!' Humdudgeon declared, staring around delightedly at all the raised hands and paws. 'Well, my dears. We've let our meeting overrun. We'll never make it back to the Squattings before the Curfew begins. Looks like we'll have to sleep here.' He started to unwind the rope which he had wrapped around his waist. 'I might as well make a start on that dam, before I get some shut-eye,' he said. 'Anyone want to give me a hand?'

Several of them volunteered their services, but Shoveller did not seem too keen to help.

'If you don't mind,' said the badger, 'I think I'll sneak a look around and find some good places to start those escape routes.' He trotted out of the chamber when his big black nose had told him that the way was clear, and his friend Fleet the fox padded after him.

For the next few days, each of the seven conspirators toiled away without complaint. The Low Gloam sentries did not know that anyone was breaking the Curfew because the little group hid themselves away and did not return to the Squattings until after they had done a night's work in their usual jobs. If they left the

Squattings before the Honks sounded it was possible to stay out for the whole day without the alarm being raised because the guards never bothered to check that every hole in the Squattings was occupied. It was tough carrying out their normal duties at night and working towards their escape in between naps during the day, but the thought of the marvellous reward at the end of all their hard graft kept their spirits high.

Shoveller was put in charge of tunnelling. Given the size of his workforce and the number of animals who would need to be evacuated, he came to the decision that two tunnels would be enough. Their codenames were 'Sweet' and 'Heavenly' which, according to Shoveller, were the two words which best summed up what fresh air smelt like. Knowing that the entrances to Sweet and Heavenly would need to be in places that were rarely stumbled upon, he chose their locations with great care. Sweet was started in a tunnel that culminated in a dead end and Heavenly was begun in another abandoned tunnel in which there had been several cave-ins. Fleet and Rusty were assigned to dig Heavenly, and Shoveller took on the challenge of Sweet. He selected MacTavish as his burrowing partner, realising that the over-eager terrier needed someone who would keep an eye on him (from time to time the dog's enthusiasm got the better of him and he started to dig in the wrong direction).

In the first day or so, they made good progress, but as

234

time went on and they drew closer to the surface, the Confining Spell seemed to get stronger as if it had a mind of its own and sensed what they were aiming to do. It was not long before their forepaws felt weak and heavy as if great weights had been attached to them and the volume of earth that they managed to shift grew less and less.

'Don't be disheartened, workmates! It means that we've almost reached the topsoil,' the badger told his team.

The actual building of the dam was undertaken by Humdudgeon with Athene and Huffkin on hand to help out as best as they could (neither was experienced at using tools). The first thing that Humdudgeon did was to nail a number of ropes to the roof of the cave. By the time that he had finished, the latticework of ropes resembled a cat's cradle pattern. Next he made himself a bosun's chair, which was a seat made from a plank of wood, suspended from several ropes. It could bear his weight and that of his bag of tools and he was able to move up and down on it to reach new overhangs of rock. He made a similar chair for Athene and Huffkin to use and during the night Athene would sit there by herself, chipping away at the rock with a chisel and a hammer. On her own, she was unable to achieve very much, but when all three of them worked together, the dam's height increased, albeit it very gradually. Just before a chunk of rock became parted from the wall, they would secure it with a net of ropes and, using a pulley which Humdudgeon had rigged up, they would transport it over to the right hand archway and lower it into the water.

Athene learned, early on, that it was pointless to break off small rock fragments. Instead of sinking to the bottom of the river and staying put, they were sucked along by the current. To build a sturdy dam, Athene, Huffkin and Humdudgeon had to concentrate on removing large chunks of rock or long, dense stalactites which would lodge themselves on the riverbed and not be dragged downstream. The job seemed endless.

Athene divided her time between working in the cave and sleeping in the hole that Shoveller had dug for her. As a fugitive, it was vital that she should stay out of sight which meant that she could not visit Zach at regular intervals, as she had promised him she would. This troubled Athene a good deal and she was both elated and relieved when Huffkin agreed to call on Athene's brother in her stead. It was through these daily visits from Huffkin that Zach first learned about the planned escape attempt.

'He's chuffed to bits,' said Huffkin to Athene as they shared a supper of ant egg broth, 'and he promises to keep it a secret – even from Tippitilda. He crossed his heart and everything.'

Another of Athene's duties which Huffkin was obliged to undertake was the writing of the Low Gloam's history book. Her handwriting was not as neat as Athene's had been, but it was deemed to be of an acceptable standard and as soon as she had finished renovating the mosaics, Huffkin was summoned to Lodestar's residence and told that she had been chosen to fill the position of scribe. In the space of a very short time, Huffkin got to know Dimpsy quite well. Ever since the day that Athene had got caught with the Book of Spells and managed to avoid being slung into the Coop, Lodestar had been in the foulest sort of mood imaginable. Unfortunately for Dimpsy, the Chief unloaded all her pent-up fury on her only servant. Bearing the brunt of Lodestar's displeasure took its toll on Dimpsy and she began to spend less time on her chores and a larger part of her day in the study, pouring out her troubles to Huffkin, who was naturally very sympathetic.

'Dimpsy looked so tired tonight,' Huffkin would say to Athene while they worked side by side in the cave, and, 'Lodestar works her to the bone, you know,' and 'I found Dimpsy in tears today. Lodestar keeps finding fault with every single thing she does.'

All of the conspirators laboured very hard, but eventually it reached the point when the diggers had done everything they could. They had got as close to the surface as the spell would allow and each pair had hidden the entrance to their tunnel by scraping a heap of dirt into the opening of their hole and flattening it to make seem as if it was a part of the wall. Having done their job, Shoveller and his team were frustrated by the painfully slow progress of the dam builders.

To keep them busy, Humdudgeon assigned the diggers another task. He asked them all to spread the word about the escape attempt to those who could be relied upon to be discreet. Humdudgeon was keen for most of the animals and Gloam who weren't in the Low tribe to be forewarned about the flood because it meant that there would be far less panic when it all kicked off.

'How many nights have we been below ground?' asked Athene not long after suppertime as she and Huffkin sat together on the bosun's chair and tapped away at a lump of rock.

Huffkin tried to recall the number of scratches that Humdudgeon had made on the wall of their hole in the Squattings. 'Nine,' she answered.

'That means my parents go home the day after tomorrow,' Athene said. 'How long do you think it will take for the dam to be finished?'

'I don't know,' said Huffkin, swinging her legs idly. 'A week . . . hmm . . . or maybe two.'

'By the time that we get out of here they'll be long gone,' Athene said. She sighed gloomily, and gave her chisel a bash. The hammer that she was using was too light to make much impact. It was the sort of hammer that Athene's mother sometimes used in the kitchen when she wanted to break up slabs of homemade toffee. Her mother's toffee was quite hard on the teeth, but it wasn't as solid as rock.

'It's going to take for ever with these rubbish tools,' she said. 'What we really need is dynamite.'

'What's dynamite?' asked Huffkin.

'It comes in sticks,' said Athene. 'When you light one it blows up. It's a dangerous explosive, first invented by a Swedish guy, I think. I've only ever seen it used in cartoons on the telly, but I reckon it would dam our river in *seconds*.'

Huffkin stopped hammering. She laid her tools on the plank beside her.

'What's up?' asked Athene, taken aback by her friend's behaviour.

Huffkin said nothing. She appeared to be thinking very hard.

'Where are you off to?' Athene said when Huffkin reached for the nearest rope and started to climb up. Without a word of explanation as to where she was going, Huffkin got to the top of the rope, swung like an orangutan across the ceiling and disappeared up another rope which led to the chamber above.

About an hour later, Huffkin returned with a package in her hand.

'You've been gone ages,' complained Athene. 'Humdudgeon was awfully cross about you shooting off like that. He was worried about you being out after the Curfew. You must've cut it very fine. What's this?' Athene said, holding up the small, square parcel which Huffkin had just dropped into her lap.

Huffkin gave her a big, broad smile. 'Remember when you were Lodestar's scribe? You mentioned to me that you'd heard an explosion and we worked out that Lodestar must've botched a spell. You told me that Dimpsy was ordered to clear up the mess she'd made. Well, I've just been to ask Dimpsy if she could remember which spell it was and sneak me the ingredients.'

'And Dimpsy agreed?' Athene asked in disbelief.

'She certainly did,' said Huffkin, smiling proudly. 'We've become quite pally, you know. She's awfully fed up with Lodestar. I told you how much she picks on her. It's Dimpsy's way of getting her own back, I think.'

Huffkin and Athene beckoned to Humdudgeon and he made his way painstakingly across the cave to join them. It was rather a squeeze on the plank.

'This is stupendous!' he declared when Huffkin had told him what the packet contained. He collected all their tools together and put them in his bag. 'We needn't bother with any more hammering,' he said, which was music to Athene's ears.

They decided to put their plan into operation the

powders to the casting of the spell. He also had to generate a far bigger explosion than the one which had happened accidentally in Lodestar's room. He aimed to make a large hump of rock above the archway drop down into the water, but it was touch and go whether he could get it to fall in exactly the right place.

While Humdudgeon was occupied with his perilous task in the cave, the others milled about in the chamber above and discussed the roles that they would be adopting in a short while. Athene's job was to fetch her brother from the Digs and Tippitilda from the Stints; the two foxes and MacTavish were responsible for guiding all the animals, reptiles and bugs into the tunnels and making sure that no one got left behind; Shoveller was entrusted with rescuing the captives in the Coop; Humdudgeon had the job of scaling the shaft with the aid of a rope and a grappling hook and helping the Gloam to climb to safety and it had been left to Huffkin, who, they had all agreed, was the most persuasive member of their group, to try to talk Lodestar into breaking her secret spell.

'I shan't shout at her or use threats,' said Huffkin as she tried to decide which tactics to employ.

'Best not to,' agreed Athene. 'Lodestar's terribly pig-headed and she doesn't like to lose a fight.'

'I'll butter her up. Yes, that's a good plan. Flattery always works wonders,' said Huffkin, sounding more confident. 'I'll tell her what a staggeringly brilliant

very next night on the seventeenth of August. For t
rest of that day, final preparations were made: ropes we
removed from the cave roof, ready to be stowed in a ho
near to the shaft; and once they had eaten their breal
fast, the escape committee were called together an
reminded of their duties which they were to carry out a
soon as the flood began. Lastly, Humdudgeon advise
them to get as much sleep as they could in the nex
twenty-four hours. At midnight the following evening
they planned to blow up the rocks in the cave below.

Athene hardly slept a wink although she tried very
hard. She remained in her little hole all night and all day,
fretting and fidgeting and imagining what it would feel
like when she stepped out into the fresh air again. She
tried her hardest not to think about what would happen
if Lodestar decided to be awkward and refused to break
the spell.

It was lonely sitting in her hole in the dark. It might
have been less of an ordeal if she had put some Goggle
Drops in her eyes, but the dribble of liquid in the
bottom of her bottle was all that she had left and she did
not like to waste it. Athene lost count of the number of
heavy sighs she gave. She longed for the evening to
come.

Humdudgeon masterminded the explosion. It wa
quite a tricky thing to get right because it depended o
him doing everything wrong; from the mixing of tl

magician I think she is. I'll go into raptures about the Confining Spell and I'll say that I'm sure no other Gloam in the world would be clever enough to reverse it.'

'And what if that doesn't do the trick?' asked Athene.

Huffkin shrugged her shoulders. 'I'll get down on my knees and beg,' she said, trying to give the impression that she wasn't worried about her forthcoming challenge, 'and if that doesn't win her round . . . oh, I'm sure I'll think of something!'

'It's fairly crucial that you do,' said Athene, wiping the brave attempt at a smile from Huffkin's face.

The blast, when it came, sounded like a colossal clap of thunder. It was far louder than everyone had expected. Unused to noises of the ear-splitting kind, the animals fared worst of all. Rusty and Fleet darted under the cart, MacTavish barked for all he was worth and Shoveller tripped over his own paws and landed in a heap.

Smoke came pouring through the hole in the floor and Humdudgeon emerged a few seconds later, coughing and spluttering and covered from head to toe in dust.

'That should do it,' he croaked.

They waited for the smoke to clear. Then Huffkin knelt beside the hole and took a good look down it.

'The water's rising awfully fast,' she said.

'Then we'd better get going,' Humdudgeon said. 'Action stations everyone!'

'Wait a minute,' Athene said, before they all charged

out of the chamber. 'What's the matter with Shoveller? I think he's hurt himself.'

The badger seemed embarrassed to be stared at by everyone. 'I'm as right as rain,' he assured them groggily. 'It was that ruddy explosion. Made me fall a bit awkwardly, and I bashed my head. Hurts like billy-o but it won't slow me down.' He teetered forwards to show them that nothing was amiss and almost collapsed in the process.

'Hell's teeth!' Humdudgeon muttered, gripping his head in his hands. 'We'll have to carry you in the cart. This throws a spanner in the works and no mistake.'

'Poor old you,' said Huffkin as she lifted the buckets out of the cart and helped to heave the injured badger into it.

Rather than acting hard-done-by and forlorn, Shoveller writhed around in frustration. 'The prisoners! What about the prisoners?' he kept saying.

'Shoveller was meant to go to the Coop,' pointed out Fleet.

'Well, someone else will have to go instead,' answered Humdudgeon.

They all stared at each other in dismay. None of them were in a great hurry to volunteer. The Coop was a long way from any of the escape routes and whoever took on the challenge would have to deal with Scabbler before they set the prisoners free.

'I'll go,' said Athene.

'You jolly well won't,' Humdudgeon said. 'Don't talk nonsense. It's far too dangerous.'

Athene's face grew very hot. She stuck out her bottom lip. 'Why shouldn't I go?' she said. 'Nobody else wants the job and, besides, I'd like to be the one to rescue Coney and Kit. I feel very badly about leaving them here and I'm not afraid of Scabbler if that's what's worrying you. It would give me the greatest pleasure to wipe that horrible smirk off his face.'

'I can't permit it,' said Humdudgeon, shaking his head. 'What if something happened to you? How would your brother cope without you?'

'He'd probably be better off,' remarked Athene bitterly. 'You think I'm a lovely sister, don't you? Well, I'm not! Zach didn't get here by accident – I told him to get inside the hollow tree because I hated him . . . because I didn't want him hanging round me any more. I'm going to the Coop,' she said defiantly, snatching up her rucksack and some rope. 'Humdudgeon, I want you to look after Zach. You'll see that he's the *first* one to get out, won't you? *Promise* me.'

'Yes, of course. I promise,' said Humdudgeon. 'I'll fetch him myself.'

Stunned by her confession, nobody moved to stop her as she turned and ran out of the chamber.

Chapter Eighteen

Waters Dark and Deep

The tunnels were teeming with bodies. Everyone had heard the blast and they were all trying to find out what could have caused it. Some of the Gloam were friendly and made room for Athene to run past, but there were plenty from the Low tribe, too, and when they caught sight of Athene, they tried to catch hold of her and some of them even gave chase.

She managed to keep up a steady pace, despite having to lug her heavy rucksack, which Huffkin had helpfully filled with all of Athene's belongings. She carried on past the Latrines and the Stints until there came a point when she thought her lungs were going to burst. Athene stopped and sank to her knees, wheezing. Expecting a Low Gloam to catch up with her, her heart filled with dread, but when she looked behind her there was no one there. A lone trickle of water snaked towards her down the middle of the passage. Faster than any of the escape committee had predicted, the floodwaters had reached the tunnels. On the one hand, this was good because it seemed as if their arrival had distracted her Low Gloam pursuers. On the other hand, it was worrying because it gave Athene even less time to complete her rescue mission.

As she leaned against the tunnel wall, trying to catch her breath, she heard screams and shouts drifting down the tunnel from the direction she had just run. Although many of the cries must have been coming from those who had been warned about the possibility of a flood, it appeared that prior knowledge was not going to stop them from getting in a flap.

Her chest heaving at a slightly less frenzied rate, Athene watched as the trickle of water swelled into a tongue shape and stretched along the ground, threatening to lick her heels. The sight of it gave her enough of a shock to make her move on. She didn't really run so much as lurch along, drawing in air in enormous rasps. After taking a few wrong turns, she eventually reached the flight of steps which led down to the Coop.

Her legs were feeling weak and wobbly, but she stumbled down the steps as quickly as she could. All was quiet. The soil was dry beneath her feet and, glancing behind her, she saw no sign of water seeping down the steps. Athene reckoned that she could afford to let herself rest for a minute while she considered the best way to tackle Scabbler. At their last meeting, she had almost floored the Low Gloam jailer with a punch to the guts and a kick in the shins. It was unlikely that the same tactics would work so well again. This time, the jailer would be ready for her flying fists and nifty footwork. Scabbler wasn't a burly man, but he was tall for a Gloam and she doubted whether she would be able to get the better of him in a fight without the element of surprise or some secret weapon. What could she utilise on this occasion?

Athene sat down on the bottom step and took off her weighty rucksack. Not really expecting to find anything amongst her belongings which would help her, she opened the rucksack's flap and delved inside it. Her fingers pushed past a woolly cardigan, a toothbrush and a bar of soap and she took out her torch and the small metallic ball which Dottle, the old Humble Gloam, had given to her. Athene had forgotten to ask Humdudgeon and Huffkin if they knew what the ball was supposed to do. Dottle had seemed to suggest that the ball could come in useful. Holding the ball by its leather strap, Athene examined it closely. It matched the size of a snooker ball, but its surface was dull rather than shiny. Athene had noticed that the ball sometimes emitted a delicate whirring sound, almost like a cat's purr, but it was silent now. She was sure that the ball held some sort of secret, but without knowing what it was, it was as good as useless to her. She dropped the ball into her lap and turned her attention to her torch. It was small, but solid and might serve as a weapon if she took a careful enough aim. Throwing objects at another human being did not really appeal to her though; especially not since she had learned about the so-called Battle of Barnyard Bedlam. Her forefinger settled on the button which switched the torch on. Force of habit made her want to press it, but she managed to stop herself in time. With her night vision enhanced by Goggle Drops, the brightness of the torch's beam would be intolerable.

A smile crept on to Athene's face. Stuffing Dottle's ball into the pocket of her trousers, she left her rucksack on the bottom step, and throwing the coil of rope over one shoulder, she stood up. It did not worry her unduly when she found that the wooden door ahead of her would not budge when she pushed her weight against it. Gripping her torch in one hand, she smote on the door with the other. She knocked loudly enough to be heard, but in a stuttering rhythm so that anyone who heard it might be fooled into thinking that the person at the door was of a nervous and non-threatening disposition.

'Oh, goody – a visitor,' said an unmistakable, whiny voice on the other side of the door. She heard muffled footsteps. Then Scabbler spoke again a little louder. 'Who is it?' he wheedled. 'Who's there? Which little lovey-dovey dinkums has come to pay me a call?'

Athene's stomach was churning. Of all the Low

Gloam that she had met, Scabbler was the one she liked the least. He was spiteful and unctuous and the mere sound of his reedy voice was enough to make her skin crawl.

Mustering her courage, Athene piped up, 'It's me, Athene. Please let me in. I'm hungry and thirsty and I'm tired of hiding. You were right. There's no way out of here. I might as well give myself up.'

There was a disconcerting hissing noise, which Athene guessed to be the jailer's self-satisfied snigger. Then she heard the sound of a bar being lifted and the door was opened a smidge. The bulbous, unblinking eyes of Scabbler peered through the narrow gap and his lips sprang apart to reveal a ghastly grin.

'Ah, my pretty one!' said Scabbler, a hank of hair falling over his face like a ribbon of slimy seaweed. 'I shall be only too delighted to invite you into my chamber, but before I do, you must promise that you will not strike my poor old bones again. Such a rude, pugnacious little madam you were at our last encounter.'

'I promise I won't hit you,' said Athene, and she meant it. Stealthily she slipped her torch into the waistband of her trousers.

Scabbler stared at her appraisingly; then nodded and opened the door a bit wider. Despite Athene's assurances that she would not set upon him, he hovered just out of her reach as she trod into the chamber. Then, without warning, he pounced.

'I'll take that,' he said, seizing the coil of rope that she had slung over her shoulder. Before she could stop him, he had tugged her left arm into a painful position, twisting it behind her back and pressing her hand between her shoulder blades.

Athene squealed and almost lost her balance as he pushed her further into the room. 'Ow! There's no need to be so rough,' she grumbled, fearing that Scabbler might break her arm if he yanked it any higher. 'I'll do what you want, all right? Please let go of me.'

'Not likely, my pet,' said Scabbler, his mouth a hair's breadth from her ear.

She did not dare to struggle while he held her so tightly, but she did manage to grab a corner of a blanket with her free hand as they shuffled past the jailer's bed.

Scabbler's constantly swivelling eyes immediately saw what she had done. 'That was very sneaky,' he said in a disapproving way. 'I'm afraid I can't let you take that blanket into the Coop. What would my other guests think of me? I can't be seen to show favouritism, can I? You must sit and shiver like the rest of them, my sweet.'

He twisted her arm even more cruelly so that Athene was forced to bite her lip to stop herself from crying out.

'Drop it, there's a good girl,' Scabbler advised her as they stumbled together across the floor like some clumsy four-legged creature.

The pain that flared in Athene's arm was agonising but, stubbornly, she refused to let the blanket fall. It was only when they were a few paces away from the hole in the floor that she considered doing what the jailer had asked.

'Drop it, I said!' snarled Scabbler, his spit spraying Athene's cheek.

'All right, I will, if you insist,' said Athene with a glint in her eye. Instead of allowing the blanket to slip through her fingers and crumple on to the floor; she tossed it over the grating which covered the entrance to the Coop.

Scabbler was taken by surprise. 'What the . . . ? What did you . . . ? ' he stammered.

Flamboyantly, as if she were unsheathing a sword, Athene whipped the torch from her waistband; then she squeezed her eyes closed, thrust the torch in the face of her tormentor and switched it on.

His shriek was so blood-curdling that it almost made her feel sorry for him. Athene suffered too, but to a far lesser degree. Unlike Scabbler, she was standing behind the torch's beam and had shut her eyes before it had appeared. The light that filtered through her eyelids was a hundred times weaker than the dazzling blaze that must have met the jailer's protuberant eyes.

In the Coop, the prisoners remained unaware of what was going on. The blanket was thick enough to shield them from the light and, as Athene had intended, they were spared any discomfort.

Athene felt the jailer release her arm, and she gave a gasp of relief. While the pain ebbed away slowly, her mind raced ahead to what she must do next. Two seconds later, however, she was startled out of her musings when Scabbler's fists made contact with the torch. A number of random blows rained down on it before Scabbler got lucky and knocked the torch from Athene's grasp. She heard the clunk and clatter as it fell to the floor. The hazy glow which had been visible through her eyelids gradually dimmed until it was dark enough for her to open her eyes. Scabbler lay on the floor with his hands pressed over his eyes. He was cursing and wailing and kicking his legs like a child having a tantrum.

'Oh, my eyes . . . my eyes! The pain! You've blinded me! You callous, vicious, hard-hearted girl! I'll have my revenge. Just you wait. I'll make you wish you'd never been born!'

With no way of knowing how long it would take for Scabbler's sight to recover, Athene worked quickly. She snatched up the rope that Scabbler had taken from her and, using a knife that lay on a nearby table, she cut the length of rope in three. Using the two shortest portions of the rope she attempted to tie the jailer's hands and feet. This was, by no means, an easy thing to do because he lashed out at her whenever he felt the rope brush against his skin. Knowing that she needed to immobilise him while she could, Athene refused to give up. Once she had tied the final knot, she left the jailer struggling against his bonds and hurried over to the Coop. She dragged the blanket away from the hole and heard voices calling out to her.

'What's happening up there?' said an anxious female voice.

'Scabbler, you're an awful brute!' declared someone else. 'We heard that poor maid screaming. What have you done to her?'

'Throw us some food, whoever you are!' said another voice plaintively.

'My name is Athene,' she called down to them. 'I'm from the Gargantuan tribe.' She was tempted to be honest and reveal that she was a Glare, but she needed the prisoners to climb out of the hole as quickly as they could and if they knew this, they might take fright and refuse to cooperate. 'I'm a friend of Coney's and Kit's,' she told them, 'and I've come to rescue you.'

This announcement prompted a great deal of murmuring.

'Did you say that you were Athene?' said an excited voice.

'Yes!' answered Athene. 'Watch your heads, everyone. I'm going to lower a rope.'

'It is her! It is!' squeaked the voice at a pitch that was

almost inaudible. 'I told you it was! Didn't I say that she wouldn't forget us?'

'Coney, is that you?' Athene said, peering into the deep hole.

'That's right – and Kit's here, too. We're very glad you've come.'

One by one, the prisoners emerged, starting with the smallest. A resourceful Gloam fashioned a sling from an item of his clothing and attached it to the rope. Three rabbits (including Coney and Kit), a mole and a rat were pulled out by this method. Then came the turn of the Gloam. The first to climb to freedom was a Nimble Gloam called Nibs who, despite his half-starved appearance, was able to help Athene heave the next Gloam from the hole. They continued in their efforts until the fifth Gloam to be rescued announced that he was the last. The prisoners were overjoyed to be out of the cramped, uncomfortable cell and when Athene told them about the flood, the news scarcely seemed to upset them at all.

'If everything goes according to plan, you'll be able to get above ground,' she said, heartened by the thrilled looks she received when she shared this information. 'You must leave here right away and run as fast as you can to the shaft. My friend, Humdudgeon, will be waiting there for you.'

'Strikes me that some of us will need a helping hand,'

said Nibs and he bent down to pick up the rat who nipped his finger indignantly and scuttled out of reach.

'I'll get there using my own four paws, thank you very much,' said the rat.

Nibs ignored the beads of blood which were oozing from his finger and tried to coax the rat closer. 'Ruffian, mate – you won't stand a chance. Use your head, for goodness' sake.'

'This is no time to get high and mighty,' Athene told the rat sternly. 'The water will be far too deep for you. You might not like the idea of being carried, but you'll have to swallow your pride, I'm afraid.'

'Never!' said the rat brazenly, sticking his nose in the air. 'Water doesn't worry me. I'm an excellent swimmer,' – and with those words, he scampered through the open door.

Nibs sucked the puncture marks on his finger and gazed at the empty doorway. 'Stubborn old git,' he said. 'Well, I s'pose I'd better go after him.' He broke into a run, giving the others a cheery wave before he vanished out of sight.

The other animals were rather less wilful than the rat had been. They allowed themselves to be picked up with hardly a murmur of protest. By now, Coney and Kit were used to being handled and the other rabbit was far too afraid of being swept away in a maelstrom of water to make any fuss.

The mole seemed the keenest to hitch a ride. He scurried over to Athene as fast as his stubby legs would carry him and clambered into her cupped hands. His body felt like a little velvet beanbag and his pointed snout kept touching her skin as if he were planting grateful kisses on her fingers.

'Let's get out of here,' Athene said, herding everyone towards the door.

An outraged screech made her stop in her tracks.

'Go ahead and save yourselves, that's right!' said Scabbler savagely. With his hands still tied together, his attempt to shake his fist at them meant that both fists were raised at the same time. 'Leave me to perish in a watery grave, you unfeeling upstarts! Well? What are you waiting for, you cowardly scoundrels? Get going!'

Athene had forgotten about Scabbler. He had ranted and railed while she had been busy rescuing the prisoners from the Coop, but when she had started to explain about the flood he had suddenly gone quiet. She had glimpsed him out of the corner of her eye as he rolled into all sorts of positions, trying to stand up; but with his feet tightly bound, he had found it impossible to keep his balance for very long (his most recent vitriolic outburst had been delivered on his knees).

'Take care of this little fellow, would you?' said Athene, transferring the mole into the hands of the person standing next to her. She smiled at the four remaining

Gloam and the furry creatures that they held in their arms. 'Now, go quickly,' she told them, 'and make for the shaft.'

'I hope you all drown,' bawled Scabbler as they rushed towards the door, 'or at the very least catch horrible colds and have to stay in bed for a year.' He made a last-ditch attempt to get up, fell on to his side and groaned with frustration.

'Aren't you coming?' said a voice from the doorway, and Athene looked up to see Coney's anxious face peeping over the arm of the last Gloam prisoner to leave the room.

'Yes,' she promised. 'I'll be right behind you. Off you go.'

As much as she despised the Low Gloam jailer, Athene could not leave him to drown. Neither could she bring herself to untie the ropes that bound his limbs. He had threatened to get even with her and, knowing what a nasty piece of work he was, she could easily believe that he would keep his word.

'Have pity!' said Scabbler when Athene approached him. He looked into her eyes so she knew straight away that his sight had returned. 'Untie me!' he pleaded pathetically as she seized his elbow and hauled him to his feet.

'There's no way I'm letting you go free,' Athene told him. 'I can't trust you to behave. I suppose I could loosen the ropes around your ankles. You won't be able to walk very well, but I'll help you.'

'Of all the petty-minded wretches! Do you really expect me to toddle all the way to the shaft in these shackles? I'll do myself an injury!' he said.

'*Oh*, stop complaining and come *on*,' said Athene, guiding Scabbler towards the door. With every second that they wasted she knew that their journey would be that bit more difficult.

Dirty, foaming water was streaming down the steps when they came out of the chamber. Athene bent down to pick up her rucksack which was half-soaked with water and heavier than it had been before. She put her arm around the jailer's waist and together they tackled the steps.

The going was tough. At the top of the steps, they both agreed that they needed a rest, and they had not made much progress up the tunnel when Athene felt like stopping again. She was drenched from head to toe thanks to the great splashes that Scabbler made every time that he shuffled forward, and her shoulders ached with the double burden of the jailer and her heavy rucksack.

'We mustn't stop for long,' she said as they both leaned against the tunnel wall. Athene was only too aware that the water was rising fast. It had been ankle-deep when they had started out, but in less than a quarter of an hour, it had risen so swiftly that it was now swirling around their knees. Another thing that she had noticed was her worsening eyesight, and this was the real reason why she had suggested that they should pause for a moment. As every second passed, the tunnel became darker and Scabbler's face more indistinct. She knew that she would never make it to the shaft before her sight failed totally. She would need to replenish her eyes with Goggle Drops.

Hastily, she shrugged off her rucksack and fumbled inside it. The bottle was in a side pocket. She eased the cork from its neck and held the bottle above her head. She was just about to tip its meagre contents into her eyes when the bottle was dashed from her hands with such force that it smashed into the wall and broke.

'My Goggle Drops!' Athene shrieked.

She was too appalled to do anything but stare openmouthed at the jailer. Just visible in the deepening gloom, she saw his skinny arms groping in the water and watched as he retrieved a shard of glass. Using it like a knife, Scabbler rubbed it against the ropes which bound his hands and feet. Then, without a backward glance, he bolted up the tunnel.

Athene was furious with herself. She had misjudged the jailer badly. She should have known that Scabbler would be far too concerned with saving his own skin to be bothered with wreaking revenge on her.

As she splashed unsteadily after him, her surroundings grew darker and darker.

In her disoriented state she turned one way and then another until she was not certain that she was facing in the right direction. It was the stupidest thing she could have done.

'Which way to the shaft?' she said. 'Oh, which way should I go?'

Confusion turned to despair as her sight failed completely and everything went black.

Chapter Nineteen

Above and Beyond

In the darkness Athene's hearing was sharper. No one answered her plea when she asked which way she should go, but if she listened carefully she could detect a sound that was different from the lapping, tinkling noises of the water as it pushed and swelled. The new noise was familiar to Athene. It was a whirring, whizzing sound and she found that she rather liked it if only because it took her mind off the terrible danger that she was in. She stayed where she was, while the water swilled around her knees, until she had located the source of the sound.

It took her ten seconds to work out that the insistent noise was coming from the pocket of her trousers. 'Of course!' she said as she put her hand inside and drew out Dottle's ball. The curious object vibrated in her palm. Holding it by its strap, she lifted the ball to her ear and heard an odd sort of buzzing sound. The harder she listened the more the sound seemed to separate and become a word that was being uttered repeatedly.

'Prezz,' said the voice inside the ball. 'Prezz . . . prezz . . . prezz . . . me.'

'Prezz me?' said Athene to herself, utterly bemused. Saying the words out loud seemed to clarify their meaning and she realised shortly afterwards that the ball was telling her to *do* something. 'Oh, I see,' she said. 'You're asking me to *press you.*'

She did as she had been instructed and finally she found an almost imperceptible button that she had never noticed before. When she pressed it with her thumb, the ball stopped vibrating and split rather neatly in two. The upper half slid beneath the lower half and the voice said something else, but this time it spoke more loudly and as clearly as a bell.

'Turn around, numbskull,' it said.

Athene was mystified. 'I . . . I beg your pardon?'

'You asked for my assistance, did you not?' said the voice. It sounded mildly irritated. 'Please proceed in a north-westerly direction.'

'What?' said Athene, whipping her head from side to side. No matter which way she turned everything looked blacker than ever. 'North-west, did you say? Wh . . . which way is that?'

She sloshed around in the water until she thought that she might have turned one hundred and eighty degrees.

The ball's next remark was a positive one. 'Your position is A OK. You may advance.'

The voice's tone was so domineering that she did not even think of disobeying it. It was a prim, haughty, no-nonsense sort of voice that reminded Athene strongly of Mrs Plant, her geography teacher.

'Who *are* you?' asked Athene, but the voice did not reply. It did however inform her that she was veering unwisely to the right (or in an easterly direction as the voice preferred to put it).

Even though the ball was just a voice and not a real person, Athene was glad to have its company. The idea of wading blindly through the water by herself with no one to give her any guidance was far too hideous to contemplate. Not wishing to drop the precious ball and lose it in the water, Athene raised the strap and lowered it over her head so that the ball banged against her chest. As she struggled through the river water (which had almost reached to the top of her legs) she wondered how Dottle could have made a helpful talking device from a simple thing like a clock.

'What time is it?' Athene said, thinking that the ball should be more than qualified to answer this particular question.

'Continue on this bearing,' was all that the ball said.

'You sound a bit like the satnav that my dad's just bought for his car,' said Athene. 'Satnav is short for satellite navigation, just so you know.'

The ball did not seem interested.

'My geography teacher, Mrs Plant, disapproves of hi-tech gadgets,' said Athene, unfazed by the ball's unwillingness to interact. 'She thinks they're bad for the brain. She's making us learn how to use a map and compass –' Athene's mouth snapped shut before she had finished her sentence. She remembered what Dottle had said about 'the Glare thingy' that she had found in a field. Apparently, it had had 'pointy bits that twiddled round and round'. 'Daft old woman,' Athene said fondly. She cupped the ball in her hand. 'You're not a clock: you're a *compass*, aren't you? You were once an ordinary compass until a Gloam got hold of you and added a little magic.'

She saw straight away why Dottle might have wished to own such a useful instrument. The old woman's night vision was poor and it made sense to have a talking compass to help her find her way home if she ever exhausted her supply of Goggle Drops.

'Do not divert from your given route,' warned the compass coldly.

'Sorry,' said Athene, and altered her direction.

When she rounded the next corner, a great swell of water rushed to meet her and almost knocked Athene off her feet. Now that the water level had reached waist height she was finding it much more difficult to press forward and the weight of her rucksack did not help. She knew that swimming would be necessary shortly and there was no way that she would be able to manage it with a heavy bag attached to her back – so, with a pang of regret, she decided to remove it. The water gave a gurgle as the rucksack dropped into its depths. Not long after she had ditched her baggage, Athene started to swim.

The current was not strong and she made good headway, but her journey became more perilous. Every now and then, her arms struck floating debris, which had once been the Low Gloam's possessions, and twice she had to claw her way through mounds of earth where the weakened walls had collapsed. With the compass underwater, Athene was obliged to submerge her head to hear its directions clearly. She tried not to panic, but she knew that her hopes of reaching the shaft were fading fast.

'Are we nearly there?' she asked desperately and, for once, the compass answered her.

'That would be correct,' it said.

Cheered by this news, Athene kicked harder and quickened her stroke. Her heart lifted again when she heard the sound of voices up ahead.

'Hi!' she called, ploughing through the water. 'Who's that? Are you in trouble?'

'Athene?' said a tired voice. 'Ouch! What was that

slap for?'

'Oh, Huffkin, is that you?' said Athene, patting the air until she found the hand of her faithful Gloam friend. 'I'm sorry, did I hurt you? I can't see a thing.'

Huffkin assured her that she was fine apart from being wet through and totally worn out. 'I've got Lodestar with me, and Dimpsy. Could you give me a hand, do you think? Neither of them can swim.'

With only the tiniest amount of resistance, Lodestar let Athene clasp her chin and pull her backwards through the water, and when Athene kicked off the floor and eased herself into her life-saving stroke, Lodestar barely struggled at all. She kept her mouth shut for a while apart from the odd grumble (mostly due to the fact that she did not want to swallow any water), but within a few minutes she seemed to get her confidence back and wasted no time in telling Athene exactly what she thought of her.

'I might've guessed that you'd have something to do with this,' she growled. 'You had "troublemaker" written all over your face. When I get out of here, I'm going to give you a dressing-down in front of *everyone*. I want them to know who it was that destroyed their homes and livelihoods. How a Gloam could do this to her own kind is beyond me . . .'

In order to keep Lodestar's face above the water, Athene had to swim on her back, which meant that her ears were submerged. The Chief's irate ramblings sounded garbled and muffled, whereas the voice of the compass was crystal clear when it told her rather smugly, 'You have reached your destination.'

Athene let her feet sink to the floor. She was the tallest of their group and could just reach the ground with the tips of her toes. Even then, her head was the only part of her to poke above the surface. From the sound of panicky breathing and splashes to her right, she guessed that poor Huffkin was having to tread water and support Dimpsy at the same time. 'Hold on to me,' Athene said, and she felt hands grab on to her shoulders.

The shaft was invisible in the dark, but Athene could sense the immense vastness of the space above her head and her nose was able to discern a freshness in the air. Athene could also hear the voices of Gloam giving orders and chanting 'heave' as they hauled their compatriots up the shaft. Athene hoped with all her heart that the deserted tunnels she had just made her way through were a good sign and that the evacuation had gone smoothly and without any loss of life.

'The spell is broken, isn't it?' Athene said cautiously. She was almost too afraid to ask.

'Yes,' said Huffkin, and from her weary tone of voice, Athene guessed that persuading Lodestar to undo the enchantment had been anything but easy. 'She wouldn't listen to reason,' said Huffkin. 'Not until Dimpsy pulled the front door open and all Lodestar's things began to float away.'

'Priceless heirlooms . . . irreplaceable . . .' muttered Lodestar grumpily.

'We only just managed to save the right powders and whatnot before the walls caved in,' said Dimpsy. 'If she had left it a minute longer to tell us what she needed to undo the spell . . .'

'It doesn't bear thinking about,' said Huffkin with a tremulous sigh.

'Don't blame me. I thought you were bluffing,' snapped Lodestar irritably. 'A flood in the tunnels? Whoever heard of such a thing? Preposterous load of old twaddle, that's what I thought it was and anyone else with a shred of good sense would have made the same assumption.'

'Everybody could have *died*,' Athene said.

'It might have been the best outcome,' said Lodestar melodramatically. 'Who knows what horrors are waiting for my tribe Up There. Once the Glare get hold of us, they'll probably tear us to pieces.'

Resisting an urge to let go of the Chief and leave her to flounder in the water on her own, Athene gave an angry tut. 'Oh, don't be so ridiculous!' she said. 'They'll have a marvellous time Above. It's a paradise compared with down here. The Glare aren't going to hurt you. I'm one myself, as I've told you before.'

'Pah!' said Lodestar. 'That's poppycock, that is.'

Athene did not think that there was any point in arguing. She was just about to ask if the women had seen her brother and could confirm that he had escaped when a stout sort of stick hit her right in the face. Athene raised her hand to brush it aside, but changed her mind and seized it instead when she realised that it was a rope. There were more slaps on the surface of the water as another two ropes were thrown down to them.

'Humdudgeon! Humdudgeon!' called Huffkin excitedly. 'We're here. There are four of us. I think we're the last!'

The answering shout came immediately. 'Huffkin! Thank the moon and stars! I'd almost abandoned hope. Is Athene with you?' He cheered when she answered in the affirmative.

'Tie the ropes around you! We'll pull you up!' he yelled.

'There are only three!' called Huffkin.

There was a change of mood at the bottom of the shaft when they were told that three ropes were all that Humdudgeon had.

Huffkin set about tying a rope around Lodestar and another around Dimpsy; then while the two Gloam were being hoisted from the water, Athene and Huffkin argued over who should have the third rope. Each thought the other deserved the right to be rescued first. Meanwhile the water rose up past Athene's chin.

'I'll tell you what,' said Huffkin. 'Why don't we go together? Neither of us is exactly fat. I'm sure Humdudgeon's team of rescuers will be more than capable of lifting us both.'

As quickly as they could, they tied the rope around their chests and tugged on it to show that they were ready. Then they heard a chorus of voices shouting, '1 . . . 2 . . . 3 . . . Heave!' and they were lifted from the water. Athene was not worried about being suspended in the air. It was thrilling to be minutes away from freedom.

Then disaster struck.

Instead of rising upwards they dropped sharply, and dangled for a second or two. Huffkin gasped and Athene feared the worst. There came a cracking sound as the rope snapped in two and they fell.

Athene could have cried with disappointment. Her body was not the only thing to tumble downwards. Her heart was also plummeting at the thought that in a second or two she would be plunged into the water again.

Then something punched her in the belly and she felt all the wind knocked out of her. She struggled as a scabby arm slithered round her waist and tightened its grip.

'What is it?' she said, then shuddered with horror when she realised that the 'arm' around her waist was a rubbery old tree root. She heard Huffkin give a shriek, and knew that the same thing had happened to her.

'Nasty old tree! It's going to take us back down,' said Athene, striking the roots with her fists. 'Its horrid roots will probably hold us under the water and drown us!'

'No! You're wrong. It's taking us up!' said Huffkin in an awestruck voice, and Athene stopped attacking the tree when she became convinced that her Gloam friend was right. The root that gripped Athene raised her up and released her at the very same moment that another root took hold of her.

'Didn't I tell you that I'd never met a bad tree?' said Huffkin, laughing with relief.

The safe deliverance of a Gloam and Glare was the very last gesture that the tree ever made, for as soon as Athene and Huffkin had been dropped on to solid ground and had staggered out of the gash in the hollow tree's trunk, it gave a terrible groan and began to lean to one side. It was night-time Above, but the dawn was close to breaking and the sky was just light enough for Athene to glimpse the huge hollow tree begin to keel over. Slowly, and with dreadful cracks and creaks, it toppled to the ground. Athene heard the thumping sound of people running across the grass. There were screams and someone shouted, 'Watch out, Scabbler!' The roots were ripped from the earth and shivered for a moment before becoming still. Then the titanic tree met the ground with a reverberating thud.

'Well done, Humdudgeon,' she heard someone say. 'You saved that foolish fellow's life, though why you bothered to risk your neck for a Low Gloam is beyond me . . . Yes, that's right, madam. Humdudgeon pushed that silly chap out of harm's way, but it's what I would expect of him. He's the bravest Gloam in my tribe, you know . . .'

'Pucklepod, is that you?' said Athene, squinting at the features of the man who had just spoken.

'Indeed it is,' he said, and she felt her hand being shaken. 'What an achievement, Athene! My, my . . . but we're proud of you. We've kept a watchful eye on this tree ever since you disappeared into it and I'm jolly glad we did. I wouldn't have wanted to miss this moment. It's an historic day! Have you ever seen so many Gloam together in one place? Tribes have come from far and wide to see this spectacle.'

It certainly seemed as if news had travelled fast. Athene tried to estimate the number of Gloam who had gathered in the field. There were too many pairs of gleaming eyes to count so she gave up. Among the tribes were some who had come to greet their long-lost members who had been incarcerated in the ground for months and, in some cases, years. Pucklepod pointed out the various huddles. 'See, there's the Nimble tribe and those hefty-looking chaps are Horny-handed, and the lanky lot by the hedge are the Gargantuan . . .'

'It's like a great big Gloam jamboree!' said Athene, grinning widely. She tried to seek out Zach and her friends in the melee, but without her Goggle Drops she could not manage it. She had fleetingly smiled at Humdudgeon, but just as she was about to speak to him he was whisked away, hoisted on to someone's shoulders and paraded around the field as a hero.

'I *must* find *Zach*,' said Athene determinedly, but before she could take a single step she felt someone tugging on her sleeve.

'Hello dearie,' said an elderly voice. 'I see you're wearing my what-d'you-call-it. Tell me, was it of any use?'

'Yes, Dottle,' said Athene, squeezing the old woman's arm and smiling. 'It was a lifesaver, actually.'

'In that case, dearie, you had better keep it. I don't quite know what went wrong with the spell, but the result wasn't quite what I'd intended. It turned out to be too bolshie by half. I never could get on with it.' Dottle patted Athene's cheek. 'I'm pleased for you, dearie. Never doubted you for a second. The Low Gloam were no match for a young lass with spirit, eh?' She grinned, dug her walking stick into the ground and hobbled away.

'Why did you save the Low Gloam?' asked Pucklepod, drawing Athene to one side. 'Why didn't you leave them down there, the vile, inhuman wretches?'

Athene tried to explain to Pucklepod that there were good and bad amongst the Low Gloam, as there were good and bad in every tribe and in every nation in the world – as there was good and bad inside herself. No one on the escape committee had even thought to suggest that the Low Gloam would not be allowed to escape with all the rest. Pucklepod stroked his beard, but said nothing. Then Huffkin appeared at Athene's side.

'They've lost their home,' said Huffkin to her chief. 'They'll need our friendship from now on, not our enmity.'

'Oh, very well,' said Pucklepod, scratching his head and frowning. 'I suppose we can offer them a place to stay until they can find somewhere new to settle down – but just don't expect me to be nice to them.' The two Humble Gloam began to discuss where the Low Gloam could be housed and Athene seized the chance to drift away and look for Zach.

During her search, she happened upon Shoveller who was trying to avoid having his head bandaged by a well-meaning Gloam. When Shoveller saw Athene, he gambolled over to greet her (nearly knocking the Gloam first aider flying).

'We did it!' he said. 'Got everyone out – even Midget the beetle! Just take in a snoutful of that air. Doesn't it smell amazing?'

Athene enjoyed the sensation of a cool breeze on her face. 'Sweet and heavenly,' she said. 'You were right.'

She moved on to talk to MacTavish who was leaping around like a puppy. When he heard that Athene was looking for her brother, he offered to help in the search.

'But then I must be off back to my folks,' he said. 'They're early risers, the Winstanleys. Won't they get a surprise when they hear me barking outside their back door?' Envisaging this happy scene clearly brought the dog much joy. His tail was causing such a draught that Athene was certain that her damp clothes would be dry in no time at all.

Eventually, with the terrier's help, she found her brother amongst the Low Gloam. He was sitting contentedly on Tippitilda's lap. He looked bright-eyed and full of life, and the instant he caught sight of Athene he sprang to his feet and took her hand.

'I've been ever so worried,' he said. 'I thought you might not find me. Tippitilda said I wasn't to go off by myself. It would cause too much bother. She said you'd come if we sat in one place and waited.'

'She's a very wise person,' said Athene, smiling warmly at the woman who had taken such good care of her brother for the past two weeks. The part of the field to which she had come was filled with Low Gloam. They stood very quietly with stunned expressions on their faces and looked about them in wonder. Athene remembered that Above was an unexplored world to them; a place that they had never set eyes on before.

'It's too big,' said one.

'I like it,' said Tippitilda.

'It's not at all how I imagined,' Dimpsy remarked. 'It's a hundred times cleaner and a thousand times more beautiful.'

Lodestar was the most dumbfounded of them all. She sat on the ground with her feet stretched out in front of her and stared and stared. From the look on her face, Athene guessed that the Chief was both perplexed and enthralled. She did not appear to be angry any more and neither did she seem to remember that she had threatened to scold Athene in front of the entire Low Gloam tribe.

As the sky grew lighter, the animals peeled away from the crowd. Shoveller trundled off to Moggy Wood, excited to hear about his new relatives ('I'm a great-grandpa, am I? Well, fancy that!'); Rusty and Fleet slunk away to find a home which would be the right sort of environment in which to raise a litter of cubs in the spring; Coney and Kit and the other rabbits disappeared into the hedge and started work on their new burrow and the little mole dived underground, happy in the knowledge that he could resurface any time he chose.

The number of Gloam dwindled too. They left the field in gaggles until only the Humble and the Low tribes were left. The sky was getting lighter with every minute and at any moment the first rays of the sun would filter past the horizon. Athene realised with a sinking heart that the time had come to say goodbye to Huffkin and Humdudgeon.

They were all too upset to say very much. There was lots of sniffing and brandishing of handkerchiefs and lingering looks and suffocating hugs.

'We'll be back next summer,' Athene promised them.

She and Zach stood side by side and watched their friends rush off to catch up with the tribes who were walking together across a distant field. Huffkin ran with a light step as if her toes were barely touching the grass and Humdudgeon sprinted beside her with only the merest remnant of a limp.

The last two Gloam to cross the country lane and join their tribe were two Low Gloam and, in the stillness of the early morning, Athene caught a snatch of their conversation. 'She really *is* a Glare, you know,' Athene heard one say, and she breathed in sharply as she recognised Lodestar's squat, dumpy figure and short, ash-white hair, 'and they're not so *very* evil as we all thought they were.'

'Time for us to wend our way, too,' Athene said to Zach.

They walked across the fields, safe in the knowledge that the compass would keep them on course. Zach thought that its voice was hilarious and deliberately strayed from their path so that the compass would be rude to him. After such an eventful night, it wasn't long before he started to drag his feet. 'I'm tired, Eeny,' he said.

The old Athene would have grabbed his hand and pulled him along impatiently, deriving pleasure from making him wail in protest. She shuddered at the memory of her former self. Feelings of hatred no longer flooded through her veins. She felt as if a curse had finally been lifted.

Athene stopped and gave Zach's hand a squeeze. 'Want a piggyback?' she asked him.

With Zach's arms draped around her neck, they made their way homeward. Dawn broke as they walked. Having been confined to a monochrome world in which colour had no place, the burgeoning hues of pink and peach and brightest blue were breathtaking.

'Will Mum and Dad still be there?' said Zach.

'Yes,' said Athene. 'They leave this morning. Pucklepod sent a Humble Gloam to lift the spell that they cast on them. They won't even know that we've been missing. It's been quite a holiday, hasn't it, Zach?'

'Oh, yeah!' he said. 'It's been the best.'

Athene was still laughing at her brother's assessment of the most dramatic two weeks of their lives when they turned into the driveway of Freshwater Farm. Crumbs, the Stirrups' tabby cat, who'd been sitting on a fence post, jumped down and ran towards them.

'I wonder what she'd say if she could speak,' said Zach. '"Where on earth have you two been?"'

'"Hurry up and give me my breakfast,"' said Athene, 'probably.'